Marta Pacini

CONSPIRACY

Disturbance Press

First published by Disturbance Press in 2022

ISBN 978-1-9168713-2-8

An early version of the beginning of this book was published in *New Writing North West 2021* (Litfest, 2021).

A CIP Catalogue record for this book is available from the British Library.

Editing by Bodhi Hunt and Charley Sixsmith.
Proofreading by Michael Clark.
Author picture by Bodhi Hunt.
Cover design and typesetting by Marta Pacini.

Cover image adapted from Ryszard Andrzejowski / Pixabay and Gordon Johnson / Pixabay.
Spine images adapted from Clker, Mohamed Hassan / Pixabay and IconsPNG.
Social media icons by iconsdb.com and Rebin Infotech / iconfinder.com.

The quote on page 184 is from Joan Smith's book *Down With the Royals* (Biteback Publishing, 2015). All efforts have been made to reach the copyright holder.

Printed and distributed by IngramSpark.

disturbancepress.co.uk

Conspiracy, n.
(1) the activity of secretly planning with other people to do something bad or illegal
(2) collective noun for a group of ravens
(see also *unkindness, n.*)

SUNDAY

"The Ravenmaster, Your Majesty."

Queen Isabel studied the man in front of her, trying – and failing – to recall their last meeting. No fault of her own, she decided: the Crown and the various royal palaces employed far too many people for her to recognise them all by sight. Besides, this man looked utterly unremarkable: average height, average build, average pink bald patch on his head. Though, as Isabel watched him straighten from his bow, she fought to suppress a chuckle. There *was* something remarkable about this man after all: an abnormally large and crooked nose, which reminded the Queen, rather appropriately, of a raven's beak.

"Please, have a seat, Mr—" What was the man called again? Isabel glanced around for her equerry, but Major Phillips was already on the other side of the gilded white door, pulling it shut. He was a recent appointment, and the Queen made a mental note to admonish him later for the ineffective introduction, made worse by the fact that her private secretary had been too busy with Whitehall matters to brief her for this appointment.

"Forgive me," the Queen told the Ravenmaster, "I seem to have forgotten your name."

"Maloney, Your Majesty. Cameron Maloney." For some reason, the Ravenmaster had remained standing.

"Of course. Please, have a seat, Mr Maloney," Isabel repeated briskly. "Apparently you told my staff that you absolutely needed to see me, and I was happy to oblige, but you should know that my afternoon was busy enough to begin with. So, what is the matter?"

Finally, Maloney took a seat on the richly upholstered chair facing the Queen's, smoothing down his coat as he did so and casting his eyes to the floor. His hand remained on his coat, and he spent several seconds fiddling with the belt buckle, looking down all the while.

"I hope it's nothing ominous," the Queen added, forcing her lips to extend into a smile and her fidgety toes to still in her stiff brogues. She had intended to reassure the clearly nervous Ravenmaster but achieved the opposite effect: Maloney pursed his lips, drew a shaky breath, began "Your Majesty ..." then stopped again.

"Now you really have me worried," Isabel frowned. "What is it?"

Maloney lifted his eyes to the Queen's face, then dropped them again. "Nero has left, Your Majesty," he murmured eventually.

"Nero? I take it you're not referring to the Roman emperor?"

"No, ma'am. Nero is one of the ravens."

"Oh? And how long has Nero been missing, then?"

"I'm afraid I haven't seen him since early yesterday morning, ma'am." As if on cue, three distant chimes rang through the open window.

Isabel considered this information for a moment. "Mr Maloney, I don't mean to be rude, but why have you come to me for this? I was under the impression that the ravens were at liberty to fly throughout the Tower grounds and beyond. Wasn't one of them spotted outside an East London pub, once?" The anecdote had been the subject of the

Queen's dresser's conversation for two days running, until Isabel had grown bored of it and had snapped at the woman to move on to another topic already.

"That's right, ma'am," Maloney sighed. "The ravens *are* free to fly around. They even leave for a day or two, sometimes."

"Then what exactly appears to be the problem?"

The Ravenmaster looked at the Queen and swallowed visibly. "The problem, Your Majesty, is that another raven did exactly that, about a week ago. Florrie. Flew out across the Thames, and I haven't seen her since. When a raven is away for that long, we have to presume the worst."

"I see."

They remained in silence for perhaps half a minute as Isabel studied the floral silk patterns on the antique-pink wall fabric, her mind already drifting towards matters more pressing than avian movements. At last, the Queen caught herself and gave her head a slight shake, forcing her gaze back to the Ravenmaster.

"Forgive me, Mr Maloney, but what is your point, exactly?"

Maloney cleared his throat. "My point, ma'am, is that this could be an ominous sign."

Isabel's eyebrows shot up. "Don't we keep spare ravens, precisely to avoid the omen you're talking about?"

"Only one, in recent times, Your Majesty." The Ravenmaster dropped his gaze again. "With Florrie gone, and now Nero, the spare raven has left. There are only five ravens left in the Tower."

"I see." Isabel looked at Maloney, who was sat rigidly

upright in his stiff-backed chair, yet somehow slumped at the same time – as though his years of military training were only partially managing to mask his dejection. His head was lowered as far as his starched collar permitted, his eyes cast down, almost as if the Ravenmaster were offering his own head to the Queen in reparation for the loss of Florrie and Nero.

"Now, Mr Maloney," Isabel said as she reached for the thick leather-backed notebook which rarely left the antique coffee table next to her favourite chair, "I appreciate your concern, really I do. But these are birds. They fly. Either we keep them caged all day, or we take the risk that occasionally one might leave. Or two, as the case may be."

Maloney made as if to speak, but the Queen silenced him with a raised hand. "I'm sorry," she continued, "but I have an urgent matter to attend to. Please replace the ravens. That will be all."

Isabel rang a bell, and the door was opened for the Ravenmaster, who stood, bowed his head, murmured "Your Majesty," and inched backwards out of the room. By the time he was out of her sight, Isabel's mind had already moved on to more pressing concerns.

* * *

Such pressing concern was the rather bothersome occurrence of a hung Parliament. The Conservative Prime Minister, Mr Fivecoat, had started losing his voters' support not long after the start of his government five years previously, but the leaders of the other major political parties were no more popular than he was.

Unsurprisingly, last Thursday's general election had failed to establish an overall majority for any party, and the leaders of the major parties had been alternately courting and tearing into each other all weekend, to no avail. Isabel felt that the time might have come for her to take action.

As if reading her thoughts, her Lib Dem chose that moment to step into the Queen's study. Cecilia Drummond was a brisk, efficient functionary of sharp focus and equally sharp appearance. When she had first taken up her post three years or so previously, Isabel had felt affronted by Cecilia's shallow curtsies and the way she sped through protocol formalities with ill-disguised annoyance. But in time the Queen had come to realise that this behaviour was driven not by a lack of deference, but by the commendable desire to get down to business.

"Cecilia." Isabel gestured towards the chair on the other side of her desk. "What have you got for me today?"

"Not much, I'm afraid, Your Majesty," the secretary replied, taking her seat and placing a pristine leather briefcase on her lap. "Mr Fivecoat has held about four rounds of negotiations with both Ms Banerjee and Ms Aboud since the election, but neither Labour nor the Lib Dems seem willing to meet the Tories' terms for a coalition."

"Right. And what do your fellow Triangle members say?" Isabel asked.

Cecilia's eyes flicked to the ceiling and back again. "Mr Simmons is advocating 'caution and moderation'—"

"Which is to say, he is refusing to express an opinion," Isabel scoffed. "Typical Cabinet Secretary."

"Precisely, ma'am. And Mr Hill has only been the

secretary at Number 10 for a few months, as Your Majesty knows, so he's not about to suggest anything that Mr Fivecoat might dislike. Too risky for his career."

"Right," Isabel said again, twirling her signet ring around her finger. The heavy white gold ring, which had been passed down from one monarch to the next for several centuries, had been on her right hand every day since her father, the late King Aldous II, had died of a heart attack when Isabel was only twenty-two.

Four decades on the throne had given Isabel plenty of time to develop a habit of twirling the ring around her finger when she was deep in thought or needing to make an important decision. After all this time the action was as automatic and subconscious to her as breathing, but her servants never failed to notice it, and would whisper to each other with a wink, "Don't disturb the Queen right now, she's twirling".

"So," Isabel wondered, "do you believe that a Tory alliance with Labour or the Lib Dems is out of the question, at this point?"

"It appears so, Your Majesty," Cecilia replied. "Ms Banerjee is fixated on giving more power to the trade unions, of all things. She won't budge. And Ms Aboud feels the same about electoral reform."

"Hold on a minute," Isabel interrupted, "are you telling me that the Lib Dems are refusing to make a coalition with the Tories on the grounds that they want an *electoral reform*?"

Cecilia shrugged. "It's the way things have shifted, ma'am," she replied. "Labour have gone to the left again, with the Banerjee election, so the Lib Dems are making a grab for the more centrist Labour voters."

"And the Tories can't make up their mind whether they're a centrist party or a right-wing one," Isabel concluded, the ring still spinning on her finger.

"Exactly, ma'am. And until they make up their mind no-one's going to risk going into a coalition with them."

"Okay, so the coalition government option is out. What about a minority government, then? Do you think that would hold?"

Cecilia pushed her wide-rimmed tortoiseshell glasses further up her nose. "I'm not sure, ma'am. The Tories have a lead of less than one percent, and the smaller parties received a lot more votes than usual this time round. I don't think Mr Fivecoat would receive a vote of confidence," she explained.

"You think he's going to resign, then?"

Cecilia pushed her glasses up even further this time. "I think so, ma'am. I would certainly resign if I were in his position, though I'm not sure how much Mr Fivecoat and I have in common."

"You would never be in his position. You're far too driven. You'd have the electorate wrapped round your finger, and if not, you'd persuade Labour *and* the Lib Dems to enter into a coalition with you."

"Your Majesty is too kind." Cecilia bowed her head in a rare display of modesty, but not before Isabel had noticed the glow which her praise had bestowed upon her secretary's face. Once again, the Queen rejoiced in having appointed her to this post. Cecilia Drummond was not only ambitious, but confident enough in her own ability to rise to the top. Isabel could never imagine Cecilia using trickery or adulation to advance her career: they were both beneath her.

"What do you think we should do, then, if Mr Fivecoat does indeed resign?" Isabel asked, twirling her signet ring once again. "Ask Ms Banerjee to form a government?"

Cecilia looked back up. "I suppose so, ma'am. That would certainly be the convention. Ms Banerjee *is* the leader of the opposition, although not by a large margin at this point."

"You *suppose* so. And what do you make of Ms Banerjee? I never warmed to her, myself. What was her slogan again? '2001: A Space Odyssey?'"

"'Back to the Future'." Cecilia grinned. "Not exactly enticing, is it, ma'am?"

"Indeed. So, what do you think of her?"

"An old-school Marxist, by all accounts." Cecilia shrugged. "I didn't know we had any of those still knocking about. Definitely didn't think one of them would end up being elected the Labour leader, but then again I've never understood the Left."

"You don't sound any more taken with Ms Banerjee than I am," Isabel observed.

"No, ma'am, I'm not. She doesn't strike me as practical-minded enough to be an effective Prime Minister. Too much of a visionary."

"I think you might be right, there," the Queen agreed. "So, the question remains: what shall we do?"

Cecilia took a breath and opened her mouth as if to speak, only to close it again. Isabel sensed her hesitation. "What is it?" she asked. "It's not like you to hold back, Cecilia. If you've got something to say, then say it. It's what you're paid to do."

"Yes, ma'am." Cecilia nodded in an almost-bow. "I was thinking, what does Your Majesty think of Harold Stone?"

"Harold Stone?" The Queen mulled the name over. "It rings a bell, but I can't place him."

"He's the MP for Wimbledon. Chair of the all-party parliamentary group on small enterprises. He spoke at that business awards event that Your Majesty opened last December."

"Oh, yes, I think I remember him. Short fellow, grey hair, looked a bit lost?"

"That's the one, ma'am. He's the leader of the Enterprise Party."

"The Enterprise Party?" Isabel repeated. "Never heard of them."

"Not many people have, ma'am. They're a small bunch, but they've managed to grab a couple of seats." Cecilia extracted a sheet of paper from her briefcase and placed it in front of the Queen.

"*The Enterprise Party,*" Isabel read out loud, "*champions the rights of individuals and their businesses. We exist to safeguard personal liberties, economic freedom and local governance. We are proud to preserve the great British tradition of true liberalism.* So," she asked Cecilia, "what are you suggesting?"

Before Cecilia could answer, the shrill tone of her mobile phone filled the air. The secretary looked at the Queen, who nodded her permission for Cecilia to take the call.

"Drummond," Cecilia snapped, rising from her chair with a distracted curtsy and inching backwards towards the door. She had scarcely left the room when she reappeared in the doorway, pocketing her phone as she bent her knees again. "Your Majesty," she announced, "the Prime Minister would like to see you."

* * *

Alan Fivecoat was one of those grey-haired, rectangular-spectacled, middle-aged White men whom Isabel had privately started to think of as 'nondescript'. As Queen, Isabel met scores of people – Members of Parliament, members of the Armed Forces, staff, the general public – and this particular mould of man was ever-present. Whitehall was filled with them. Her own staff was brimming with them too – which was probably why Isabel had been so keen to appoint a younger person, and a woman at that, as her new private secretary a few years previously.

Nondescript Man found a lifelong companion in Nondescript Woman, of course – equally White, short hair dyed blonde, spectacles slightly larger than her husband's, perhaps in a shade of purple or sporting a few sparkles near the hinges. But, for some reason, her existence had never bothered Isabel as much as that of her male counterpart. Perhaps this was because her favourite lady-in-waiting, Lady Gillian Swanson, who had served Isabel ever since the start of her reign, was the prime example of Nondescript Woman.

Isabel had grown up surrounded by women like her – quiet and dignified, happy to serve and remain in the background – whereas the only men she had really known in her childhood were her relatives, who all stood above and apart from the nondescript masses by virtue of being royals, if nothing else.

"Prime Minister." The Queen smiled graciously, gesturing towards the nearest chair as she considered that this was probably the last time she would address Mr Fivecoat in this way.

The Prime Minister bowed, and as he lifted his head again and took his seat the Queen was reminded of one of the reasons why she had never thought much of the man: the annoying nervous tic he had. He would squeeze his right eye and then his left, giving his head a small shake as he did so, which had earned him the nickname of 'Twitchy Alan' in the press. It was cruel, she recognised, to think less of a person because of an involuntary reflex such as this; but she was the Queen, after all, and who could indulge in a bit of harmless cruelty to spice up her routine, if not the monarch?

"Your Majesty." Mr Fivecoat cut into her thoughts. "I'm afraid I come to you with glum news."

"How so?" Isabel asked politely, though the answer wasn't hard to guess.

Mr Fivecoat took a shaky breath, his eyes darting towards the floor again. "I am here to ..." Another shaky breath.

Isabel took pity on the man. "Would you like a drink of water, Mr Fivecoat?" she offered.

"Yes, please, ma'am," Mr Fivecoat rasped.

Isabel stood up to fetch the water herself from a tray on the sideboard, causing the Prime Minister to jump frantically to his feet. He took the proffered glass with trembling fingers and another bow, resumed his seat once the Queen had taken hers, took two long gulps of water and started again.

"Ma'am, I am here to tender my resignation as Prime Minister of Your Majesty's government," he managed in one rushed breath.

"Oh? What a shame," Isabel offered. "I take it the negotiations didn't go well, then?"

"Not well enough, Your Majesty. I'm afraid the leaders of the other major parties seem to think that some of their principles are incompatible with a coalition with us." Mr Fivecoat's eyes were twitching faster than Isabel had ever seen.

"I suppose principles are something of a double-edged sword, when it comes to politics," the Queen remarked.

Mr Fivecoat frowned. "Yes, I suppose Your Majesty is right."

"So, what are you going to do now?" Isabel asked with a smile. Mr Fivecoat looked so sad that she decided to fetch them both a brandy, not even bothering to ask first if the Prime Minister - *no,* former *Prime Minister,* the Queen corrected herself - would like one. He clearly needed one, and it's not like she hadn't seen him drink alcohol before.

Once Mr Fivecoat had stood up in surprise again and accepted his drink with another bow, he sank back into his chair and let out a sigh. "I'm not sure, Your Majesty," he finally answered. "Probably take a long holiday with my wife, somewhere sunny. Then, I don't know. I'll find something, right?" he asked with a nervous laugh. Isabel wasn't sure whether he was posing the question to her, or to himself.

"Mr Fivecoat, you're a former Prime Minister." He winced at those words. "Of course you'll find another job. You'll have your pick. Now, if you'll excuse me, I have a lot of work to do, as you can imagine."

The Queen stood up again, and this time she didn't sit back down until Mr Fivecoat had left the room, bowing and scraping, for the last time.

* * *

"Mum!"

Isabel had been about to call Cecilia back into her study to continue their conversation about Harold Stone when her son Alexander barrelled into the room, nearly crashing into the side of the door frame. He propped himself up against it with an outstretched hand and stood silent and panting for several seconds.

Isabel lifted an eyebrow. "Prince Alexander Edward Louis, you are no longer five."

At her acid tone, Alexander remembered himself, peeled himself off the door frame and bowed his head, huffing and puffing all the while. "Sorry," he wheezed. "It's urgent. And important." He shoved a sheet of paper into Isabel's hand, then planted his hands on the tops of his thighs and stood there, slightly hunched over, until Isabel motioned with her head towards an armchair.

The Queen watched her son fold his long limbs into the chair. He was not five, but thirty-five, with the muscular build and permanent tan that came from having spent two decades running between tennis courts, polo pitches and racing boats. Isabel could not remember the last time she had seen him with untidy hair, his shirt rumpled and half-untucked. He must have been running extremely fast to lose his breath, fit as he was, and Isabel examined the document he had thrust at her with concern.

It consisted of two sheets of white paper, crumpled and creased; they had clearly been folded to fit into an envelope, which presumably now lay somewhere in the vicinity of Alexander's desk. The top-left corner of the front sheet sported a flag with yellow, blue, and red horizontal stripes, the middle stripe studded with white stars, and an elaborate coat of arms in the same colours. Next to these symbols, two lines of large, bold letters proclaimed *Gobierno Bolivariano de Venezuela – Ministerio del Poder Popular de Petróleo.*

Isabel, who during her time at Wycombe Abbey had thought French the only foreign language worth the attention of a future queen, squinted at the string of unfamiliar words for a few seconds, before realising that the Spanish had been translated into a smaller heading underneath: *Bolivarian Government of Venezuela – Ministry of Popular Power for Petroleum.*

The letter bore last Thursday's date and was simply addressed to 'Alexander, Duke of Cornwall', the customary 'HRH' having been undiplomatically left off. The body of the letter was short and painfully unceremonious:

Sir,

It has come to my attention that PetrIsland Corp., a company of which you are the majority shareholder, has been colluding with other petroleum refineries in Singapore to suppress the price of crude oil, to the detriment of crude oil exporters such as Petróleos de Venezuela, S.A. (PDVSA). I am duty-bound to remind you that PDVSA and its subsidiaries are the property of the Bolivarian Republic of Venezuela. Any action which damages PDVSA is an action against the interests of the Venezuelan people, and therefore constitutes an act of war.

I have no choice but to demand that PetrIsland Corp. desist from cartel trading effective immediately. Should your company fail to comply, the Bolivarian Government of Venezuela will be left with no choice but to take military action to protect the interests of the Venezuelan people.

Signed: HE Rafael Gutiérrez Marrero, Minister of Popular Power for Petroleum

Countersigned: HE Patricia Santiago Contreras, Minister of Popular Power for Foreign Affairs

"What?" Isabel had to read the letter a second time for its contents to fully sink in. "*What?*" she repeated after the second reading, uncharacteristically lost for words.

"Yup." Alexander had finally recovered his breath. "Two prominent members of the Venezuelan government have essentially just threatened me with war. *Us*," he immediately corrected himself, "threatened *us* with war."

"But ..." Isabel thought back through her weekly conversations with the Prime Minister over the past several months, trying to recall any references to Venezuela and its oil. She found none: as far as she knew, the United Kingdom and Venezuela enjoyed cordial relations. "Wait, Alexander – is your company really involved with a cartel?"

"No! Who do you take me for?" Alexander flashed Isabel his signature grin, and she felt her insides melt a little, the way only her son could make her feel.

"Okay. Sorry, sweetie – I had to ask."

"I know. But even if we were doing cartel trading, which we're not, the appropriate response would hardly be a declaration of war, would it?" Alexander said, a perplexed look marring his usually carefree attitude.

"Quite. I just don't understand why they would—"

"And that's not all, Mum," Alexander continued. "I was having lunch at White's the other day, and I saw Brad Carmichael-Spence. Remember him?"

Isabel thought for a moment. "That blonde boy you were friends with at school?"

"That's right. Anyway, I went over to say hello, and I

overheard the guy he was with talk about Caracas. 'Those DFs are as good as sold to Caracas,' that's what he said."

"DFs? What's a DF?"

"I don't know," Alexander shrugged. "Could be anything. But Brad's in the arms trade now, in his father's company. What if the guy was talking about missiles?"

"Missiles? Hang on, Alexander, aren't you jumping the gun a bit? No pun intended," Isabel added with a shudder.

"I don't know, Mum. But Brad's not taking my calls, and his secretary told me that he's abroad for business, when I only saw him here in London a couple of days ago. And I remember him telling me and the other guys at our school reunion that DF-41s are some of the most powerful intercontinental missiles around. They have a range of over seven thousand miles, can you imagine that?"

"Bloody hell." Isabel was not normally given to swearing, but these did not feel like normal circumstances.

"I know. And did you notice, in the letter, how they addressed me as the Duke of Cornwall?"

"Yes, but what's that got to do with anything? You *are* the Duke of Cornwall."

"I know, but I'm also the Prince of Wales, and they didn't call me that, did they? Look, Mum – do you have a map of the world?"

Isabel, feeling slightly dazed, extracted a large rolled-up world map from a drawer and spread it onto her desk, pinning its corners down with paperweights and pencil holders.

"Look," Alexander said again, moving his finger down the Atlantic coast of the Americas until he found what he was looking for. "This is Caracas, right?" he added, stopping his finger on a point on the northern coast of South America. "All they have to do is fly over a bit of the Caribbean, and then it's just international waters all the way over here." Alexander's finger traced an arc across the Atlantic Ocean and came to rest on the southern coast of Cornwall.

Expressing a desire to ingratiate himself with the people of Cornwall ahead of his investiture as their Duke, Alexander had chosen to study for his Business degree at Falmouth University. Having fallen in love with the area – and with keelboat racing – he had remained beyond his graduation from Falmouth and his investiture at Launceston Castle to oversee the renovation of a suitably princely palace on a stretch of Duchy land near Truro. He now spent most of his time in Cornwall with a neverending carousel of guests, making trips to London only when royal and business affairs demanded it, or when he tired of the local clubbing scene.

"This is bad, isn't it?" Isabel whispered. "This is really bad."

"Yeah. You need to do something, Mum."

A knock on the door interrupted their conversation, and Isabel schooled herself back into her usual composed demeanour before calling out "Come in!".

Cecilia appeared at the door. "Excuse me, Your Majesty – Your Royal Highness," she said with a shallow curtsy. "I don't mean to disturb, but we should probably continue our discussion. Time is ticking on."

Isabel gestured for her to enter the room. "Don't worry, Alexander," she smiled, waving the Venezuelan letter which was still in her hand. "Leave this with me. I'll take care of it."

Alexander flashed her his special grin again as he bowed his head, then nodded to Cecilia and left.

Isabel resumed her seat and invited Cecilia to take the chair that Alexander had vacated. "So," she began, "what were you telling me about Mr Stone?"

"I presume we are now without a Prime Minister, Your Majesty?"

"You presume correctly."

"Well, ma'am," said Cecilia, taking a sheaf of papers out of her briefcase again, "the reason I mentioned Mr Stone is that he seemed to have a good head on his shoulders, when I spoke to him at that event last winter. I've looked into him and he seems solid. Practical-minded. He's not an idealist like Ms Banerjee and some of the others, but he also seems to know what he stands for, which is more than can be said for some parties."

"And he's from the Business Party?"

"The Enterprise Party, ma'am."

"Right. Not exactly major players, are they? How many votes did they get?"

"Oh, only around a hundred and twenty-thousand, ma'am. About nought point four percent. They chose their constituencies well and got themselves a couple of seats. Stone still runs his own company on the side – something to do with missiles."

"Really?" Isabel studied the papers in front of her with renewed interest. "This might be exactly what's needed," she concluded after a few minutes. "But doing things this way would be most unusual. Some might even say unconstitutional."

To the Queen's surprise, Cecilia grinned at this. "With all due respect, ma'am," she replied, "Your Majesty forgets that we don't have a constitution."

* * *

Harold Stone took a deep breath to steady his nerves. He glanced around at the hallway walls, which were covered in solemn portraits and bucolic landscapes framed in gold, and up at the gilded ceiling. He had been in such a daze, throughout the car journey here and the several rounds of security checks, that he hadn't been able to take in his surroundings. Finally, though, he was starting to catch up with reality, and he remembered the words his wife had called out after him as he ran out the door, still straightening his tie: "I want a detailed description of the place when you come back, Harold!".

Typical Mavis, always grabbing any opportunity to enrich her knowledge of the fine arts. Harold was glad he had remembered her admonishment, though he wasn't sure how much he was really taking in. His hands were shaking, and he took another deep breath.

"Are you alright, Mr Stone?" asked the officer whose name and rank Harold had been too bewildered to absorb. Tall, broad-shouldered and as grey-haired as Harold himself, he was wearing a green-brown uniform with two aiguillettes draped over one side of his torso.

"Mr Stone?" he prompted again.

"I'm fine, thank you," Harold belatedly remembered to answer.

"Are you ready to go in?" the officer pressed. "Her Majesty is waiting for you."

Harold gulped down his nerves and nodded.

The Queen's study looked much like the hallway, with enough gold on the ceiling and antique paintings on the rose-pink walls to keep an Art History expert like

Harold's wife entertained for hours. Harold himself, however, barely took the room in – he was too consumed with the idea of being in the presence of the Queen.

The monarch was sitting in a plush upholstered chair facing the door; though the late afternoon sunlight from the window behind her made Harold squint, he thought he saw the Queen frown at him. Harold remembered himself, cast his gaze down hurriedly and bowed, feeling his face flush as he did so. He kept his head lowered for several seconds, hoping this would be interpreted as a sign of deference, rather than a botched attempt to let some of the pink fade from his cheeks.

"Mr Stone, Your Majesty," Harold heard the officer announce.

The Queen rose. "Thank you, Major Phillips," she said. Harold lifted his head just in time to see Major Phillips – *so that was his name!* – bow and retreat out of the room.

The Queen took a few steps towards Harold. "Mr Stone," she said, extended her right hand, "thank you for coming at such short notice."

Harold started to extend his own hand when Major Phillips' instructions resonated as a warning in his head. He hurriedly bowed again before shaking the Queen's hand. "Your Majesty," he murmured, breathing out a sigh of relief at seeing the frown lines distend on the sovereign's forehead.

The Queen pointed to a chair in front of her own, and Harold took it with a third bow, just to be on the safe side, clasping his hands in his lap to stop them from shaking. He raised his eyes, peeked at the Queen, and nearly opened his mouth to ask what on Earth had prompted her to summon him to Buckingham Palace; but again he remembered Major Phillips' protocol instructions containing something about not speaking first, so he kept quiet.

"I believe we almost met before, Mr Stone," said the Queen amicably. "Last December, at some business awards?"

"That's right, Your Majesty." Harold remembered that evening well: the Queen had given a short speech to open the ceremony, and shortly afterwards Harold had delivered his own, much longer keynote speech. He had been looking forward to meeting the Queen at the end of the evening, and had practised bowing in front of the mirror for the best part of a week, to Mavis's great amusement; but once he'd stepped off the podium he'd been informed that the Queen had had to leave on urgent business. For what felt like the hundredth time that evening, Harold wondered why the sovereign had seen fit to call him here now.

"I must congratulate you on your election results."

"Thank you, ma'am," Harold replied, modestly inclining his head. "Can't compete with the big guns, obviously, but we did better than I had hoped."

"Yes, well, that's why I called you here, actually."

Harold took a moment to digest these words. "Forgive me, ma'am," he ventured eventually, "I'm not sure I understand."

"Mr Stone, as you know, a hung parliament awards me a degree of involvement which I wouldn't normally have."

"Yes, ma'am," Harold exhaled, no less confused than before.

"And I must say that I find the leaders of all three major parties inadequate for the onerous task of government."

"Indeed," Harold replied before he could stop himself. A fresh wave of heat rushed into his cheeks.

To Harold's astonishment, the Queen grinned. "I see we are on the same page, there," she continued. "In light of all this, I was wondering, Mr Stone - how would you like to form a government in my name?"

Harold felt his stomach go hollow and was grateful for the chair holding him up. "I-I beg your pardon, ma'am?" he croaked.

The Queen grinned again. "I thought I'd asked you a simple question, Mr Stone," she remarked with a lift of her eyebrows.

"But ... But ..." Harold squeezed his hands tight in his lap and took a raggedy breath. "But why me, Your Majesty?" he wheezed.

"Well, it seems that you impressed my secretary at that event last year, Mr Stone," said the Queen in an even tone. "Which you should take as a huge compliment, by the way - Cecilia's not easily impressed. However," she continued, "you don't seem particularly excited at the prospect of becoming the next Prime Minister. Perhaps I should ask somebody else."

"No!" The scream escaped Harold's lips before he could do anything to stop it. He stiffened at his own boldness and scanned the Queen's face for a sign that he had gone too far, but the monarch appeared, if anything, amused.

"No, please, Your Majesty," Harold corrected himself. "I was surprised, that's all. Of course, I would love to form a government in Your Majesty's name. I'd be honoured." Images of the Tudor period dramas which Mavis was partial to filled Harold's head, and he had to fight the urge to kneel in front of his sovereign and kiss her ring there and then.

"Good," said the Queen, clapping her hands together the way Mavis did when she took a cake out of the oven and was pleased with the results. "I supposed I'd better let you get on, then. It's late. Come and see me tomorrow morning, Prime Minister."

The Queen's parting words sent another jolt to Harold's stomach, and it was a couple of seconds before he had recovered enough to stand up, bow again and take his leave.

* * *

"Sorry, sorry, sorry!" Fran panted, barging into her own house and dumping her handbag by the door. "There were delays on the Northern Line – what's new? I don't even know why we needed a stupid team bonding evening anyway. Keisha and Muhammad spent the whole time making out in a corner, and if I have to listen to one more story about Doreen's cat I swear I'm going to scream. And Dan is a really sore loser."

"Hey, breathe!" Alice said with a laugh as Fran collapsed onto a worn floral armchair. "It's alright. The boys are in bed and the laundry's all folded. Glass of wine?"

"You're a star. Go on, then, let's have a nightcap, shall we?" Fran fetched two glasses and Alice filled them from a bottle of white she had spotted in the fridge while making dinner for herself and Fran's sons.

"How were they?" Fran asked once they had sat back down. "Any fuss?"

"No, no fuss at all. They ate all their food and went to bed on time."

"Thank God for small mercies. How's uni going?"

"Fine." Alice shrugged. "I'm done with lectures now, just revising for exams. I can't wait for it all to be over."

"You'll miss it, though, I bet. I didn't go to university, but I really missed sixth form college when I started working. I always thought school was a drag, but actually it's work that's the real drag. School was a lot more varied."

Alice thought for a moment. "Yes, I probably will miss uni. I'll miss the people and the whole atmosphere. SOAS is a bit of a unique place. I won't miss the stress, though!"

"Well, you'll have plenty of stress working as a lawyer, won't you? Sorry to put it so bluntly!"

"You're right. Speaking of ..." Alice drained the last of her wine. "I'd better go and get some sleep. I've got an interview tomorrow and I don't want to mess it up."

"Oh my God, that's tomorrow?" Fran looked mortified. "I'm so sorry I kept you here so late! I would have told work to sod off if I'd known!"

"It's alright," Alice said again. "It's not that late, and I've only got to go next door. Don't worry about it."

"Thank you so much." Fran got up from her armchair and walked Alice the few steps to the door. "Are you sure I can't pay you?"

"Nah, you're alright." Alice wasn't rich – very few students are, especially in London – but between some help from her parents and her part-time job at the SOAS bar she kept herself afloat. Helping a single mother out by babysitting on the odd evening and during half term – which normally coincided with the SOAS reading week – felt like a decent thing to do. Besides, Alice had grown up around lots of younger cousins, and taking care of Ben and Milo came easy to her.

"Well, thank you again," Fran repeated. "And good luck tomorrow! I'll buy you dinner to celebrate, even if it might just have to be a takeaway from the Chinese on the corner."

"Or to commiserate," Alice pointed out.

"Deal. Although I'm sure you'll be just what they're looking for."

* * *

It had been a long day for Isabel: multiple meetings with Cecilia, Mr Fivecoat finally resigning and needing a lot of mollycoddling, Alexander's letter from Venezuela, Mr Stone wandering in and then out of her study in a stupor ... plus, of course, the million other tasks which filled the daily life of a sovereign. It was with some surprise, therefore, that as she tried to unwind and go to sleep, the Queen found herself thinking back to her brief encounter with the Ravenmaster.

Isabel knew, of course, the legend of the ravens at the Tower of London, had known it for so long that she couldn't recall hearing it for the first time, much like the story of Cinderella or the myth of Father Christmas. King Charles II had been visiting the Tower of London when he'd been approached by the resident astronomer, who had petitioned the sovereign to get rid of the ravens nesting at the top of the White Tower and obstructing his work. Advised that ejecting birds which had been at the Tower for so long might turn out to be a bad omen, Charles had removed the astronomer instead and had ordered by royal decree that no fewer than six ravens should be kept at the Tower of London at any one time. Should the ravens leave, the legend continued, the Tower would fall, and a great misfortune would befall the kingdom.

Isabel knew this story to be just that – a story, good for entertaining tourists and children, certainly not something to be taken seriously. Not only that: she distinctly recalled her father telling her, while they were visiting the Tower together, how during the Blitz most of the ravens had fled the Tower – and lo and behold, the kingdom had survived the war, had even *won* the war! So why did the Ravenmaster's words keep swirling around in her head – "there are only five ravens left in the Tower"?

I'm being silly, Isabel decided. *I've had a long day and I'm overwrought, that's all.* She rang for Lady Gillian and asked her to fetch them both some chamomile tea, and the two of them settled in for some night-time gossip. When Isabel finally fell asleep, her dreams were inconsequential and raven-free.

MONDAY

"Hey, Alice, have you seen this?"

Emery plonked themselves down on the common room sofa, causing Alice to bob upwards and spill coffee on her skirt.

"Hey!" she squealed, placing her travel mug gingerly on the floor and rooting around in her big handbag for tissues. "I was going to go to my interview in this!"

"Sorry." Emery shrugged, handing Alice a packet of Kleenex. "Your mug is the same colour as your top. I didn't notice it."

"You don't need to notice it," Alice pointed out. "I'm a final-year student, and it's May. When am I *not* drinking coffee?"

"Good point. You look very on-brand, by the way, with your SOAS mug."

"I have to. Who's going to take me seriously as an environmental lawyer if my travel mug game isn't on point?"

"Oh my days!" Emery laughed. "That can be your job interview strategy. Forget the CV and the tests. Just show up with a company-branded mug and you'll be hired."

"Great plan. I'll do that this afternoon, after I've gone home and changed, thanks to you." Alice sighed.

"So, who's this one with, then?"

"Jammer and Barrett. They're quite big in Environmental. Wish me luck," Alice shuddered.

"Aw, I'm sure you'll be great! Anyway, what I was trying to say is, have you seen this?" Emery shoved their phone under Alice's nose. It showed a BBC News web page.

"*Unexpected PM appointment puts Queen centre-stage*," Alice read out. "Wait, what?" Her eyes travelled past the headline to a picture of a middle-aged White man, grey hair receding, who looked like he had been in the middle of a speech when the photo had been taken.

She read the caption: "*Harold Stone, 63, leader of The Enterprise Party, claimed shock at monarch's decision.* Emery," Alice asked, turning wide-eyed to her friend, "are you telling me that this random guy is supposed to be the new Prime Minister?"

"Seems like it," Emery nodded. "Isn't it fucked up? I mean, his party hardly received any votes. They've only got a couple of MPs."

Alice frowned. "But how is that possible? I mean, if the Prime Minister resigns and there's a hung parliament, isn't the Queen supposed to ask the leader of the opposition to form a government?"

"How should I know?" Emery countered. "I'm just a lowly Music student. You're the future lawyer. I thought *you* would know."

Alice cast her mind back through the many courses she'd taken during her time at SOAS. "You do realise our uni specialises in Africa and Asia, right?" she reminded her friend. "I haven't studied British Constitutional Law since first year."

"Well, what did you learn in first year, then?"

Alice raised her eyebrows. "That was a lifetime ago. Let me think." Putting her coffee down again, she took a pen out of her pocket and started absent-mindedly doodling leaves and branches along the side of her hand. "Okay, I'm not sure, but I think Aishah said something about it being a convention, not the law."

"Who's Aishah?"

"My Public Law lecturer. Wait, what day is it today?"

"Monday, why?"

Alice took her phone out and tapped into it a few times. "We're in luck," she announced, "she's having office hours right now. Wait for me down here?"

"Sure," Emery replied with a glance at their watch. "I'm free until twelve. See you in a bit."

"See you!" Alice grabbed her bag and coffee mug, kissed her friend on the cheek and disappeared at speed towards the main staircase.

She ran back into the common room twenty minutes later and found Emery still sitting on the same sofa, now sipping a coffee of their own.

"I was right," Alice panted. "Aishah told me that it's all convention. I do remember this from first year – everything in the so-called British constitution is conventions. It's all 'this is how things have been done for centuries, so we're going to assume that they will continue to be done the same way'."

"I've never heard of anything more British in my life!"

"I know." Alice rolled her eyes. "What do we do, though? We have to do something. Do you know if a protest or anything has been organised yet?"

"No idea. You're the campaigns officer. I just play in the samba band," Emery laughed.

"So, because I'm the campaigns officer, and a Law student, I'm supposed to know everything?"

"Uh-huh. Why do you think I voted for you?"

"I would have thought friendship, or maybe even that you liked my manifesto, but clearly not." Alice glanced at her watch. "I've got to go and get changed for my interview.

I'll message Cora to see if SRD have anything planned. You coming to the Union meeting later?"

"Yeah, I'll see you there. Maybe you can say something during your Campaigns slot? Start to get people organised?"

"Good idea. See you in a bit." Alice gathered her things and strode briskly towards the door.

"Good luck!" Emery called after her.

"Thanks!" Alice shouted back. "I'll need it."

* * *

Harold Stone woke up disoriented in the way he usually did on his first morning away on holiday, when he would grope to his right for a glass of water from the nightstand, only to find that the nightstand was to his left, or just out of reach, or even that there was no nightstand at all. It always took a few moments of sleepy confusion for him to remember that he had travelled to a new place. That's the way Harold was feeling on this day, even though he woke up in his own bedroom, the nightstand to his right, just where it had been the day before.

Harold sat up, rubbed sleep from his eyes and tried hard to figure out why he was feeling like something momentous had happened the previous evening. Then, in a flash, the realisation gripped him that something momentous *had* happened, something so unexpected that, for a second, he wondered whether it had all been a dream: the Queen had invited him for an urgent private audience and had asked *him*, Harold Stone, just like that, to form a government in her name.

"Alright, love?" Mavis sat up in bed next to Harold and

put her arm around his shoulders. "Sleep well?"

"Yeah, eventually. Took me a while."

"I bet. Me too." Discovering the purpose of Harold's summons to Buckingham Palace had quelled Mavis's questions about the paintings and interior design, which was saying something.

"Well, I suppose I'd better get on and ... form a government." Harold shook his head. "What the hell just happened, Mavis?"

"I don't know, love," Mavis chuckled. "But, hey, don't look a gift horse in the mouth. Egg and bacon to fortify you, Prime Minister?"

"Thanks." Harold kissed Mavis's cheek as he got up. "Blimey. I still can't believe it."

Many more 'blimeys' bounced around Harold's dining room an hour later, as he told the Enterprise Party Executive Committee about the events of the previous evening.

"We'll need to find somewhere else to meet," observed Stephen Roady, the party's secretary, lightly stroking the polished glass surface of the table. "We can't hold party meetings in your house anymore, Harold, if you're going to be the Prime Minister. We'll look like a joke."

"You're the joke, dude," laughed Rob Mbuko, the party's Vice President and Harold's fellow MP. "We'll have the whole of Number 10 to meet in."

"Bloody hell, you're right!" Joanna Pearce, the communications officer, joined in. "I hadn't thought of that. Why aren't we meeting there, then, instead of here?"

"Quicker," said Harold. "And quieter, I imagine. Now, please, folks – we need to focus. I'm trying to form a Cabinet here." He pulled a crumpled envelope from his pocket. "Let's see ... Joanna, you're an investment banker – you can take on the Exchequer."

Harold heard Joanna take in a sharp breath and mutter, "I *hope* I can," but he ploughed on.

"Rob – Home Secretary. Steve – why don't you do Communities and Local Government? You're good at that stuff."

"You should give him Transport, with a name like Roady!" laughed Kim, the membership secretary.

"Ha, ha. Kim, you take Education," answered Harold, without missing a beat. "Naomi – Foreign Secretary."

"Oh, so because I'm foreign I get Foreign Secretary?" asked Naomi in her slight Nigerian lilt.

"And because you've worked all over the world."

"Fair enough," Naomi agreed.

"Rhys, you take Wales."

"Hell yeah!" whooped Rhys Madog, the party's policy officer. "Been a while since we've had a Welsh Secretary who's actually Welsh!"

Harold continued in this manner until he had filled all Cabinet positions. There were over twenty of them, and Harold exhausted all of the party's officers and most of the other regular faces. He realised with a jolt that he would have to draw on some of the party's less committed members to fill the remaining ministerial positions.

"Now what?" Joanna's voice broke into Harold's thoughts.

"Now, I'd better get myself to Number 10," he sighed. "Been avoiding it long enough. The media will be going mad," he added with a shake of his head while he went to fetch his coat. "Right, where's my press secretary?"

Silence descended upon the room. "I don't think

you've appointed one yet, Harold," Kim pointed out after a few seconds.

"Oh." Suddenly, Harold felt all energy drain from his body, and he slumped back onto his chair. He tipped his head back, closed his eyes and took a couple of deep breaths before looking up at his new colleagues again. Two dozen pairs of worried eyes returned his gaze.

"I'll do it for now, Harold," said Joanna, with a smile which was either filled with pity, sympathy or possibly both.

"Huh?"

"The press secretary thing. I'll do it until you find somebody."

"Thanks, Joanna." Harold smiled weakly. "Alright, everybody – let's get ourselves to Downing Street."

* * *

The offices of Jammer and Barrett LLP, Labour and Environmental Solicitors, were located on the grandly named Paradise Row, at the intersection of several gardens in a busy but pleasant part of Bethnal Green. Alice arrived early for her interview and headed for a bench in Paradise Gardens with a view of the office building.

As she sat trying to calm her nerves, she imagined what her life might be like if she were awarded a training contract here. She would cycle to work every day from a house she would share with two or three like-minded young professionals, perhaps still in Hackney where she lived now, on the other side of Victoria Park.

She would shower at work and change into a blouse-and-pencil-skirt combo to channel her inner Rachel Zane from *Suits*. No heels, though: her principles would inspire and inform her work, attire included, and she would silence any critics with a couple of well placed Caitlin Moran quotes. *Yes*, Alice thought – she could get used to this.

Alice hadn't gone to SOAS with the explicit intention of becoming an environmental lawyer, though she had always known that it was one of the areas of practice which attracted her the most. With a father who worked as an international law adviser at the United Nations office in Harare, and a mother who co-directed an education and welfare charity, Alice had grown up observing two opposite sets of frustrations. Her mother's resentment towards the lack of resources allocated to those who needed them the most, and her father's sense that his work consisted of exchanging a lot of lofty words and worthy opinions which, more often than not, failed to be translated into anything practically useful, were consistent themes in Alice's childhood.

Just before leaving Zimbabwe for England, Alice had become really excited about the successful struggle that a community group in Marange – which her uncle belonged to – had pitched against a diamond mining company which was operating illegally and contributing to water pollution and soil erosion. As she had learnt about more of the victories that environmental lawyers and their clients had scored over the past few decades – the preservation of the Kaiparowits Plateau in Utah, the halting of waste disposal into Lake Munyanyange in Uganda, the closing of a mining company which was creating radioactive waste in Malaysia – Alice had formed a picture of the environmental lawyer as someone who actually gets things done – for their client and for the whole ecosystem. She just had to cross her fingers that her hopes wouldn't be crushed too badly.

Alice's phone buzzed, and she saw a text from Emery with a simple thumbs up emoji. Smiling, Alice took a deep breath and headed towards the office building.

* * *

At the same time Alice entered the offices of Jammer and Barrett, LLP for her interview, Isabel was sitting in her favourite armchair, the one next to the fireplace, waiting for her new Prime Minister to arrive for a meeting. Even in May, when all traces of the last lit fire had long been swept from the hearth, this felt like the most restful spot in the palace, and Isabel knew that she had a long day ahead.

The sound of shuffling feet caught Isabel's attention, and she lifted her gaze to see Mr Stone standing by the door, head bowed, waiting for instructions. She pointed magnanimously to the chair facing hers and rang for some tea. Once the maid had been and gone, Isabel reached into the inner pocket of her blazer and pulled out the letter that Alexander had shown her the day before.

"Mr Stone, I imagine you might be wondering what prompted me to choose you as my next Prime Minister," she began.

Mr Stone did not appear surprised at this remark. "Well, yes, Your Majesty, I have been wondering that. Not that I don't relish the opportunity," he added hurriedly.

"Of course. But you were hardly the obvious choice." Mr Stone pursed his lips at this, but didn't answer, so Isabel carried on. "Would you tell me a little bit about your company?"

"My company, ma'am?"

"Yes, your company. I was under the impression that in addition to your political career you manage a military company. Or am I mistaken?"

"Yes, ma'am – I mean – no, ma'am." Mr Stone blushed. "What I mean to say, ma'am, is no, Your Majesty is not mistaken, and yes, I do indeed co-direct a company. Stone Armstrong."

Isabel thought that sounded like the name of a pub, but she stopped herself from rolling her eyes – Mr Stone seemed flustered enough as it was, and she needed him to focus. "Well, then, tell me about what Stone Armstrong does," she prompted.

"We're a ballistics consultancy firm, ma'am. We specialise in missiles – trajectories, maintenance, strategy, all of that. We advise the armed forces, mostly. I founded it with a friend from Imperial College. But Your Majesty doesn't need to worry – Patricia does most of the day-to-day stuff now. My co-director, that is. I am fully committed to my parliamentary and government duties," Mr Stone replied with a tight smile.

"Oh, I'm not worried about that. In fact, your professional background was one of the main reasons for my interest in you, Mr Stone."

"Really, ma'am?"

By way of an answer, Isabel handed Mr Stone the letter from the Venezuelan foreign ministry. As Mr Stone read, she saw the same emotions play out on his face that must have shown on hers when she'd first read the letter: surprise, disbelief, fear, anger, disbelief again.

He held on to the letter for a full two or three minutes, and Isabel saw his eyes travel up to the top of the sheet and down again at least twice. When Stone finally looked up again, his face was nearly as white as the piece of paper he was clutching.

"Your Majesty ... this ... this is preposterous, right?"

"If you're asking me whether my son engaged in illicit trading practices, of course he didn't. But there's more to this than just the letter. I have already informed the Head of MI6, and they're looking into it as a matter of extreme urgency. Alexander has reason to believe that the Venezuelan government may have recently acquired some DF-41 missiles."

"DF-41s?" Mr Stone spluttered.

"Yes."

"Bloody hell!"

Isabel sat up, startled, and must have given Mr Stone one of her withering looks, because in the space of a second she saw his face turn from white to near-purple.

"Your Majesty, I ..." he stammered. "I'm sorry, I should never ... Forgive me."

Isabel considered the situation for a moment. "Normally, I do not tolerate foul language in my presence, Prime Minister," she admonished.

"Of course, ma'am, I—"

"However," Isabel continued, silencing Mr Stone with a raised hand, "under the circumstances, I find myself obliged to agree with you. Bloody hell, indeed."

* * *

Harold – accompanied by his newly formed cabinet – was headed to his first Privy Council meeting. It was only four o'clock, but he already felt exhausted.

After the meeting at his house in Wimbledon, Harold and his Cabinet had made a brief appearance at 10 Downing Street for the press, and then he had dashed to Buckingham Palace to meet with the Queen. They had then both headed over to Parliament, where the Queen had opened the new parliamentary session with a speech about the need for new leadership in the face of the upcoming military threat.

The Queen's speech seemed to have convinced enough MPs to give Harold and his government a chance, and the required vote of confidence had been passed with a slim majority, and not without vehement opposition from the Labour Party and several independents. Immediately afterwards, in the House of Lords, the new Cabinet members had been made Peers – the obvious way for an unelected politician to become a Cabinet Minister.

The group were led to a large anteroom and left to murmur to one another in amazement and bewilderment at the sudden change in their personal – and their party's – fortune. Two figures stared them down as they entered.

"Prime Minister," Caroline Banerjee greeted Harold in an icy tone. The Labour leader was imposing: her six-foot-one-plus-heels frame towered over Harold's five foot seven, and there was something searching in her gaze that made Harold squirm like a schoolboy summoned to the headteacher's office.

Harold, whose political career had begun well past his fiftieth birthday as a bit of a joke with his mate and now fellow MP Rob Mbuko, always found himself intimidated by people like Ms Banerjee, who had been elected to the Commons for the first time at twenty-three and had taken over the Labour Party's leadership at the still tender age of thirty-nine. But then again, Harold supposed that only someone with an extremely resolute personality could have managed such a stellar career in what Harold's niece Tilly - who, to her parents' dismay, had joined Young Labour while in sixth form - described as 'a party still dominated by middle-aged White men'.

"Hello, Ms Banerjee. Honoured to meet you properly," Harold ventured with a small smile, extending his hand.

Ms Banerjee shook it but didn't return the smile. "Congratulations on your appointment," she said, her tone as sharp as the cut of her suit.

"Th-Thank you," Harold bumbled. He tried to think of something else to say to fill the silence which was already descending between them, but was rescued by the approach of the Prime Minister - *no!* Former *Prime Minister!*

"I would also like to extend my congratulations to you, Prime Minister," Alan Fivecoat drawled. The man, like Harold himself, was no spring chicken - but even so, he looked as if he had aged a decade in the past week. His cheeks were sagging, his eyelids drooping slightly, and his jacket, although clearly well tailored, looked too large on his hunched shoulders.

Fivecoat must have noticed Harold examining him, because he shrugged as they shook hands. "Don't worry, my party will get round to sacking me just as soon as they can figure out who the next top dog is going to be."

Harold felt himself blush. "Oh, I wasn't—" he started to say.

Fivecoat silenced him with a raised hand. "No offence taken. It's how it goes. Good luck to you."

"Thanks," Harold rasped, finding that his throat was starting to dry out.

"If you're wondering why Mr Fivecoat and I have both been invited to this meeting," Ms Banerjee interjected, "I expect Her Majesty couldn't make up her mind as to who should now be considered the Leader of the Opposition. Besides, there's not many people left to attend Privy Council meetings in-between governments. Though, I must say, you have brought quite the retinue with you."

Harold was saved from having to answer that last remark by the opening of the big double doors at the far end of the anteroom. Mr Fivecoat started to walk towards them, halted, turned around, stepped aside and gestured, pink-faced, for Harold to go ahead.

"Please—" Harold started to say.

Fivecoat muttered, "After you." Harold, not wanting to add to the former Prime Minister's embarrassment, was about to insist that the other man go first, when a hand on his back propelled him forward.

"Go on, Hal," he heard Rob whisper in his ear. "You're the boss now."

Harold squared his shoulders and led the way into the room, where the Queen stood waiting. As he and Rob bowed, he heard his friend whisper, "Well - maybe not quite *the* boss," then stifle a laugh. A raised eyebrow from Her Majesty ensured that Harold went beet red and nearly stumbled as he moved to make space for Mr Fivecoat, who had ended up behind Rob.

As Ms Banerjee had pointed out, theirs was a sizeable group, and they had to squeeze themselves into a tight arc to fit inside the room. This was a much plainer room than the Queen's study, and Harold, who had been expecting a sumptuous, interminable gallery in the style of Mavis's favourite Tudor films, couldn't help but feel a little deflated. *Is this what it means to be 'on the inside'?* Harold thought.

Should he be so blasé about his position in office as to consider lavishly decorated palace rooms quite beneath him? Or would he always feel the way he was feeling in this moment – somewhere between a tourist and an impostor?

"Mr Stone?" The Queen's impatient tone broke through Harold's internal musings, and from Ms Banerjee's stifled laugh he surmised that the monarch had tried to get his attention at least once before.

"Y-Yes, Your Majesty?" Harold stammered, giving his head a slight shake in an attempt to clear it.

"Have you chosen the next Leader of the House of Commons?"

Harold felt a knot form in his stomach, the way he used to when a teacher called him to the board as a schoolboy. "Of-Of course, Your Majesty," he improvised, glancing around the room at his newly picked Cabinet members and at the two members of the opposition. "It will be Mr Mbuko," Harold declared, his choice made easy by the fact that Rob was the only other member of the party to have been elected to the Commons in the first place.

"Very well. Shall we—"

"Your Majesty," intervened Ms Banerjee, "I'm sorry to interrupt, but I think there may be a procedural issue here. Mr Stone's government hasn't yet received the confidence of Parliament," the Labour leader reminded the gathering, in a tone which brokered no doubt about which way her vote of confidence would go.

"Not only that, Your Majesty," Mr Fivecoat piped up. "I know that the Leader of the House of Commons is normally also the Lord President of the Privy Council, but I don't see how my Mr Mbuko could fulfil that role before even being inducted into said Council. No offence, Mr Mbuko," the former Prime Minister added with a glance at Rob, who smiled genially.

"You both make a good point," the Queen conceded. "Mr Fivecoat, I believe you are the most senior Counsellor present. Will you act as Lord President for today?"

Mr Fivecoat preened. "I would be honoured, Your Majesty."

"Very well. Will you do the honours, then? No pun intended." The Queen gestured towards the assembled group.

"Forgive me, ma'am. I don't actually know the purpose of this emergency meeting."

"Oh, that's right. There was no time to issue a formal invitation. Well, our first order of business is to swear all these people in as members."

Harold, who was standing almost directly opposite Mr Fivecoat, saw his eyes widen, then rotate both ways to take in the whole room. "*All* of them, ma'am?" the acting Lord President croaked.

"That's what I said. This is the new Cabinet. They need to be sworn in."

"Your Majesty," intervened Ms Banerjee, "I don't believe that would be—"

"Usual? No, it wouldn't," the Queen retorted. "But I

think you'll find that it *is* constitutional, Ms Banerjee. Now, Mr Fivecoat, if you please – we have quite a few new members to get through."

At a nod from the Queen a short man in a dark, gold-trimmed uniform – whom Harold had failed to notice until this point – left his position in a corner of the room to retrieve two embroidered footstools. He placed one in front of the Queen and the second one not far behind, then approached Harold and handed him a piece of paper. Before Harold could ask for an explanation, the man returned to his position in the far-right-hand corner of the room.

Harold glanced at the paper, which listed a long series of instructions. He had only just begun to read them when he heard the uniformed man – clearly some sort of clerk – call his name. Panicked, Harold scanned the sheet of paper again, and spent a couple of seconds committing as much of the instructions to memory as he could.

"The Honourable Harold Stone!" the clerk called again with a certain pointedness in his voice. Harold walked with trembling steps towards the footstool furthest from the Queen, risked another quick glance at the now crumpled paper in his hand, and knelt.

"Hmm-hmm," a fake cough resounded. Harold raised his head again to see the clerk raising his eyebrows at him and jerking his head to the side, as if trying to point something out without being noticed. Harold glanced around himself, trying to spot the source of the problem.

"Hmm-*hmm*," the clerk sounded again. Harold, who was both left-handed and left-footed, checked himself and felt his cheeks heat up. He hurriedly lifted his left knee off the footstool and shifted onto his right, lowering his left hand and raising his right as he did so. Somewhere behind him, Ms Banerjee sounded like she was finding it harder and harder to contain her amusement.

"Harold Stone," the clerk intoned, "you do swear by Almighty God to be a true and faithful servant unto the Queen's Majesty, as one of Her Majesty's Privy Council. You will not know or understand of any manner of thing to be attempted, done, or spoken against Her Majesty's Person, Honour, Crown, or Dignity Royal, but you will let and withstand the same to the uttermost of your power, and either cause it to be revealed to Her Majesty Herself, or to such of Her Privy Council as shall advertise Her Majesty of the same.

"You will, in all things to be moved, treated, and debated in Council, faithfully and truly declare your mind and opinion, according to your heart and conscience; and will keep secret all matters committed and revealed unto you, or that shall be treated of secretly in Council. And if any of the said treaties or counsels shall touch any of the Counsellors, you will not reveal it unto him, but will keep the same until such time as, by the consent of Her Majesty, or of the Council, publication shall be made thereof.

"You will to your uttermost bear faith and allegiance unto the Queen's Majesty; and will assist and defend all jurisdictions, pre-eminences, and authorities, granted to Her Majesty, and annexed to the Crown by Acts of Parliament, or otherwise, against all foreign princes, persons, prelates, states or potentates. And generally in all things you will do as a faithful and true servant ought to do to Her Majesty. So help you God."

"I do," Harold proclaimed, feeling like it was his wedding

day all over again. Running through the instructions in his head, he stood and walked to the second footstool, making sure to kneel on his right knee this time.

The Queen, who had stood emotionless throughout the proceedings, extended her hand towards Harold, and he fancied he caught the hint of a smile as she did so. He kissed the Queen's hand, stood, took a step backwards and bowed. As he turned and walked back to his place in the semicircle, he let out a sigh of relief.

A carousel of newly appointed ministers followed in Harold's wake: kneel, walk, kneel, kiss, walk, repeat. The clerk's voice started to grow raspy somewhere around the tenth induction, but he dutifully carried on. The Queen stood expressionless throughout, gracefully extending her hand at the appropriate times. From the corner of his eye, Harold observed Ms Banerjee shift her weight from one foot to the other with increasing frequency. Mr Fivecoat, on the other hand, stood motionless and with a vacant expression on his face, as if stunned.

Once the final member had been inducted, Mr Fivecoat turned to the Queen. "What's the next order of business, Your Majesty?" he asked in a resigned tone.

"There isn't one. Thank you for volunteering to act as president today, Mr Fivecoat. Now, if you'll excuse me, I have a lot of work to do."

"Unbelievable," Harold heard Ms Banerjee mutter to Mr Fivecoat as the two of them passed him on their way to shake hands with the Queen.

* * *

"Come on, folks!" Eda Bashir, one of the co-presidents

of the SOAS Students' Union, called into her microphone. "I know it's been a weird day, but we're nearly there. Next up is an update from our campaigns officer, Alice."

Alice drained the last of her beer and stepped up to the microphone stand which had been set up at the back of the common room. At least fifty faces were looking at her from the battered sofas, benches and chairs which filled the Junior Common Room – the heart of the university.

"Comrades," Alice began, and was interrupted by a snigger from the front of the room. Following the sound with her gaze she spotted Mike Pranger, the president of the SOAS Anarchist Society, laughing into his pint glass. Alice inwardly rolled her eyes as she remembered the end-of-term party the previous winter, when Mike had cornered her in the bar downstairs and had subjected her to a half-hour tirade on why the intercollegiate group she belonged to, Students for Real Democracy, should adopt a "postmodern campaign rhetoric".

"At least we get some shit done," had been Alice's parting remark, and though she suspected that Mike might have a point, she lacked the time to find out what a postmodern campaign rhetoric might look like in practice.

"Comrades," Alice repeated, "it's been a busy few weeks for Campaigns. Thank you to everyone who has been involved in the student strikes to demand sick pay and pensions for our cleaners." A few cheers broke out at this point, and Alice waited until they had faded away before continuing.

"Next Tuesday, management are having a meeting about teaching contracts for next year, so we need as many of you as possible to send emails and tweets to the school demanding an end to zero-hour contracts. I've shared the details on the Campaigns social media pages." Alice waited again as a few people tapped into their phones or scribbled in their notebooks, hopefully making a note to take part in the upcoming action.

"But the most urgent thing is that Students for Real Democracy have organised a meeting tonight to talk about the new Prime Minister and how we might take action. It's at seven in the café on the ground floor of the Birkbeck building, just round the corner. Please come if you can, and keep an eye on the Campaigns social media for updates. I imagine things will be moving quickly."

* * *

Isabel was in the drawing room enjoying a cup of tea with Lady Gillian – which felt well deserved after such a busy couple of days – when her equerry announced that the Ravenmaster was seeking an audience.

"I spoke to him yesterday," the Queen snapped.

"I know, Your Majesty. He insists that what he has to say is both urgent and important." Major Phillips' tone was apologetic but unwavering.

"Fine." Isabel dismissed Gillian with a roll of her eyes and promised herself that she would keep the meeting brief and return to her cup of tea in no time.

Maloney was stooping, even after straightening from his bow. He clasped his hands in front of him, tightly enough to turn his knuckles white, and stood with his gaze lowered as if awaiting sentencing. His face looked grey, and Isabel noticed two deep grooves running either side of his beak-like nose.

"What is it, Mr Maloney?" Isabel asked shortly. "I've had a very long day. Has another raven flown the nest?"

Maloney's lips tightened at this, and he stooped lower, as if recoiling from a blow. "Y-Yes, Your Majesty," he mumbled. "Ness. Yesterday evening. I gave it twenty-four hours, then ran back here." Maloney's head was now bent so low that all the Queen could see was his balding crown.

"Look, Mr Maloney ..." Isabel didn't bother to repress the sigh that rolled through her. "I am an extremely busy person at the best of times, as you can imagine, and the recent situation in Parliament hasn't helped. I haven't got time to be worrying about a flock of birds, with no offence meant to you and your job. If you cannot manage to replace the ravens, perhaps someone should be thinking about replacing you."

Maloney flinched. "It's not that simple, ma'am," he replied. "With ravens being protected by law and doing better in the wild, there's only one breeding programme left, and it's all the way in Northern Ireland. We were going to breed our own at the Tower. I mean, we have – Ness was only born last year, around the time Hugh died. But now she's left, and the breeding season's already over. I've contacted the folks near Belfast, but their young won't be ready to leave the nest for another three months or so."

Isabel hadn't heard so much about birds since the time she had been asked to open a new RSPB reserve, and that had been at least ten years ago. "Listen," she snapped, her patience fraying, "it's only a silly legend, after all. I don't mean to say that it's not important – it's tradition, and this whole enterprise is built on tradition." Isabel made a sweeping gesture at her study. "But we'll live. The kingdom will live. Just do your best to replace those ravens as soon as you can."

"Yes, Your Majesty." The Ravenmaster bowed his head but didn't move.

"Was there anything else?"

"Well ... yes, Your Majesty." Maloney hesitated, and Isabel raised an eyebrow and gave him a pointed look to hurry him along. "It's a message from the Resident Governor of the Tower, ma'am. She asked me to inform Your Majesty that a large crack has been discovered in the White Tower, in the roof of the chapel apse."

"A crack!" Isabel, who had been about to take a sip of her tea, slammed her cup down on the low table instead, causing the Ravenmaster to flinch. "When has a monarch ever had the time or the inclination to worry about a crack?" Maloney started to reply, but Isabel had had enough. "Please tell the Resident Governor to do her job," she added. "Good evening, Ravenmaster."

Having settled the matter, Isabel rang for Lady Gillian again and went back to her tea.

* * *

"What kind of a weird day was that?" exclaimed Kim, always direct and to the point, before taking a long swig of beer. Harold nodded, busying himself with his own rapidly emptying bottle of London Porter, and saw several other heads bob around him in agreement.

He took in his fellow party-members-turned-ministers, who were sitting uneasily on the edge of their rigid seats around the huge Cabinet room table and thought that it felt like an age since they had gathered at his dinner table. How could only twelve hours have passed since then? And how could the Wimbledon semi that he and Mavis had owned for decades feel so enticing and yet already so remote, after a day spent traipsing the halls of the most prestigious buildings in Westminster?

"What was it like, Harold?" Naomi's voice interrupted his musings.

"What was what like?"

"Your speech in the Commons, before they voted on the Queen's. I wasn't there. I was too busy being made Lady Salbourne, remember?"

"It was fine."

"Fine!" boomed Rob from his place at Harold's right hand. "It was a mastery of political rhetoric, especially for something scribbled on the back of an envelope in the four minutes it takes to drive from Buckingham Palace to Parliament."

"Back of a Privy Council instruction sheet, actually, which reminds me that I still need to shred it. But thanks, Rob. You've always been an excellent cheerleader."

"There's an image I'll never get out of my head!" Steve intervened. "Rob in a shiny leotard, waving a pair of pom-poms in the air."

"Shut up, Roady," Rob shot back, though he was laughing along with the rest of the room.

"Hey!" Steve retorted. "It's Lord Tanham now, I'll have you know."

"I still can't believe it," piped up Rhys. "I never thought I'd be made a Privy Counsellor *and* a Peer, all on the same day. My husband's gone and told the whole family already. My WhatsApp's going mad."

"It's a mighty big injustice, is what it is," Rob replied with a theatrical shake of his head. "Hal and I work our butts off for years to get ourselves elected *and* lead the Party, and in two seconds flat you lot become the next biggest faction in the Upper House after the bishops. But if you think you can lord it over us – literally – think again! Right, Hal?" Rob concluded his mock tirade with a slight bump of his elbow to Harold's ribcage.

"It's funny," Joanna remarked before Harold could reply, "how you always call Harold 'Hal'. You're like the King, Harold."

"I think the phrase you're looking for is 'Prime Minister', Joanna," Harold frowned. "And we haven't had a king for decades. We have a queen, remember? Tall, grey-haired? We were with her this afternoon?"

"No, you knob!" laughed Joanna. "The Netflix film, *The King*. With that guy with the French name. Timothy something. Have you not seen it?" When Harold shook his head, she continued: "It's about Henry V, but his friends call him Hal. At the beginning of the film he's a bit of a fringe prince, really. His brother's supposed to succeed their father to the throne, and Hal just spends his time messing around and drinking. But then the father and the brother both die, so Hal becomes king and has to deal with suddenly having all this power and responsibility."

"Yep, that's me. Minus the messing around and drinking. Well," Harold considered, draining the last of his porter, "maybe a little bit of drinking."

"Yeah, well, it's hard to survive Westminster without a bit of drinking," said Rob. "I bet that debate about sanctioning Venezuela tomorrow is going to take forever. Couldn't you just make the decision yourself, Harold? Or the Foreign Secretary, whoever that is now."

"Me," Naomi called from across the table.

"There you go. Couldn't Naomi just impose the sanctions? I swear democracy is overrated." The volume of Rob's voice, fuelled by the two-and-a-half pints of lager he'd already swallowed, had risen as he'd spoken, and his last sentence drew a few amused gasps from the tables nearby.

"Keep your voice down!" Harold admonished him. "Do you want to give the press a field day?"

"I'm sorry to break this to you, Hal, but we're under threat from Venezuela and Parliament have just consented to a complete nobody becoming Prime Minister. No offence. The press is already having a field day."

"Fair enough," Harold mumbled into his beer. "Anyway, to answer your question, yes, Naomi could have just imposed the sanctions. But Her Majesty advised me that if I went through Parliament first it would help give this government legitimacy, both with Parliament and with the public."

"Yeah, I suppose I get that." Rob downed the last of his beer and stood up to go back to the bar. "So, we're going to have to sit through hours and hours of debate, just to give ourselves a bit of legitimacy. I still think democracy is overrated."

TUESDAY

"I got it!" Alice knew she was five minutes late for the SRD meeting, but as she approached the table where Emery was sitting she couldn't help squealing her news in their ear. Apologising for her lateness could wait.

Emery turned towards her with an exaggerated flinch. "Hello to you too. You got what?"

"The job! The training contract! From that interview I had yesterday!"

"Oh my God! Well done!" In a moment Emery was on their feet, giving Alice a huge hug and squealing as much as she was. "At that environmental place? What was it called? Hammers and Bassets?"

Alice snorted a laugh. "Jammer and Barrett, but close enough. And thanks! I'm so relieved. Look!" She held up her phone and read out loud: "*Dear Ms Mushonga, we were impressed with your application and interview for the post of trainee solicitor. We would like to offer you a place on the training programme starting on Monday 7 September*. I still can't believe it!"

"Congratulations, Alice!" Deshad, the most active SRD organiser at King's College, called out from their table. Emery had signed him and Cora into the main SOAS building, and they had commandeered one of the large wooden tables in the Junior Common Room. SOAS was always a good place to be if you were going to organise a protest – there was a near-hundred-percent chance of making recruits.

Alice dumped her bag on the table and pulled up a chair. "Hi, Cora. Hi, Deshad," she said with a sheepish grin.

"Sorry I'm late. I got the email about the job as I was locking the front door, and I swear I just stared at my phone for a full minute in the middle of the street. I must have looked like an idiot."

"Don't worry," Cora replied with a smile. "I was the same when I found out I had won as president of my SU for next year. It's so nice to know what you're going to do next."

"Tell me about it. I like having a plan."

"Speaking of plans," Deshad interjected, "shall we make a start? We've got banner-making at three."

"Yes! Sorry," Alice said again. "So, there's quite a few people from SOAS up for doing stuff. Not as many as usual, obviously, because everyone's revising for exams, but still. Should be a fair few, and hopefully we can recruit more when they see us making banners in an hour."

"And the samba band are up for playing," Emery added.

"Great! I love your samba band," said Cora. "The UCL folks are the same. Lots of people revising like mad, but there's quite a few going according to the Facebook event, and my tweets are getting lots of retweets, so hopefully it will be a decent turnout. What about King's, Deshad?"

"Same. I've spoken with some of the SRD people from Birkbeck, Queen Mary and Goldsmiths and it looks like we're going to get a few dozen people between us."

"Watch out, London! The SRD takeover has begun!" Emery mock-yelled, drawing a few stares from the rest of the common room.

"Hell yeah!" Cora joined in. "Seriously, though – I get

that there's exams coming up and everything, but this isn't just Students for Real Democracy trying to find an excuse to have a good time. This is fucking serious. How on Earth did Stone manage to get a vote of confidence?"

"I guess people get scared easily," Deshad observed. "He waved some military threat in front of Parliament and suddenly he's the bee's knees."

"I think it's the fact that he said he would resign straight after dealing with this supposed missile that convinced them," said Emery. "And if he doesn't resign they can always put forward a no-confidence motion then, can't they, Alice?"

"Yeah, that's what Aishah told me yesterday. I just refuse to accept that we could end up with a completely random Prime Minister that nobody voted for. I mean, my cousins in Zimbabwe think Britain's this beacon of democracy ... if only."

"Well, we're not accepting it, are we?" Cora replied. "That's why we're planning this protest. Let's show the good people of London that this country is a bloody joke."

* * *

"We now come to the motion in the name of the Prime Minister, to be moved under Standing Order Number 24. I remind the House that the motion is as follows: 'That this House has considered the necessity of imposing immediate economic sanctions on the Bolivarian Republic of Venezuela as a deterrent measure against offensive and unprovoked military action'. I now call the Prime Minister to move the motion."

Harold had been a Member of Parliament for five

years now and was well versed in the jargon and procedures of the House of Commons, but it still took him a couple of seconds to remember that when the Speaker of the House said "Prime Minister" she was calling *him*. He finally caught himself and rose with all the dignity he could muster.

"Thank you, Madam Speaker." Harold found that his throat was dry and cleared it discreetly before continuing. "I beg to move that this House has considered the necessity of imposing immediate economic sanctions on the Bolivarian Republic of Venezuela as a deterrent measure against offensive and unprovoked military action.

"As this House heard during Her Majesty's speech yesterday, and again when I made the application to be granted this emergency debate yesterday evening, the Venezuelan Foreign Minister and Minister for Petroleum have sent His Royal Highness Prince Alexander an extremely insulting letter alleging that a petroleum refining company of which His Royal Highness is the majority shareholder, PetrIsland Corp., has been part of a cartel aimed at suppressing the price of crude oil.

"They have threatened military action should the company fail to cease the cartel trading immediately. His Royal Highness has, of course, denied these allegations, and this government has seen no evidence that either the prince or PetrIsland Corp. have engaged in any illegal activity—"

"Of course they haven't seen any evidence!" the Labour Member for Knowsley, Mac Coatney, stood and shouted, and was echoed by a chorus of "hear, hear!" from several members of his party.

"Order!" the Speaker of the House cut in. "Resume your seat, sir." Mr Coatney sat, a smug expression on his face, and Harold had to scan his sheet of paper to find his place again.

"As I was saying, Madam Speaker, there is no foundation for the very serious allegations which the Venezuelan government has made against the Prince of Wales and his company. It is imperative that this House, and indeed this country, give a clear signal to the government of Venezuela that we will not be intimidated by their lies. And I have no doubt that the historic allies of the United Kingdom will join us in imposing sanctions to send the Venezuelan government the clear message that vile and baseless threats against the sovereignty of a great democratic country such as ours will go neither unnoticed nor unpunished."

Harold sat back down among murmurs from various parts of the room and poured himself a glass of water from the jug in front of him, a welcome perk of his new position on the front bench.

Harold knew, really, that enough MPs would support his position: after all, today's debate wouldn't be happening at all if the House hadn't passed an emergency motion the previous evening to allow the emergency motion to be tabled. Not to mention the fact that the House had only approved the Queen's speech because Her Majesty had made the threat from Venezuela abundantly clear; Harold was in no doubt that as soon as the situation was resolved he would have to resign, or face being booted out through a vote of no confidence.

However, as he had told Mavis when he'd finally made it to bed the previous night, he didn't mind. For a backbencher from a fringe party who had gone into politics as a bit of a diversion from running the same company for four decades, a few months or even weeks as Prime Minister were more than he had ever imagined possible.

Despite the support that a majority of MPs had already demonstrated for the sanctions, the debate was fierce, as Harold had imagined it would be. As the Prime Minister of a minority government – probably the smallest minority in the country's history, now he thought of it – Harold knew that he was skating on thin ice, no matter how persuasive the Queen's speech had been.

Caroline Banerjee and most of the other Labour MPs, as well as several Fivecoat loyalists, put up a considerable fight, arguing that the Venezuelan attempt at intimidation need not be taken seriously. Harold couldn't shake the impression that what they really meant was that *he* should not be taken seriously.

In the end, however, the same sense of urgency and indignation at the threat of foreign military action which had prompted the majority of Members to approve the Queen's Speech prevailed again, and the motion was passed.

A much lengthier debate then followed to discuss and amend the emergency bill that Harold, Rob and a few of the Downing Street staff had spent much of the previous night drafting. By the time the bill had been read twice, debated, read a third time and finally approved, Harold was exhausted; he and Rob took one look at each other and dragged themselves off to the Sports and Social Club to meet the rest of the Cabinet.

"Bloody hell," Steve grunted as he lowered his considerable frame into a chair. "These sessions are worse than my mother when she gets started about her petunias. I haven't been this bored since school. How did it go at your end, guys?"

"Only slightly more exciting than yours, by the sound of it." Rob shrugged off his jacket and slung it on the back of the chair opposite Steve's. "Hal got shouted at by a bunch of Reds, but that's about it. Drink, Prime Minister?"

Harold managed a nod and a grunt, and Rob sauntered off to the bar. Joanna, who had just returned from the Ladies', went to sit next to Harold and shot him a concerned look.

"Are you alright, Harold?" she asked in the same tone he had heard her use with her children when they came along to Enterprise Party Christmas dos.

"Yeah, I'm fine." Harold smiled weakly. "Just knackered, you know? And there's still so much to do. We haven't got even the skeleton of a political staff force, for one thing."

"I know." Joanna patted Harold's arm, returning his smile. "One thing at a time, eh? Let's get this sanctions bill sorted out first."

"Yeah, you're right. Speaking of ..." Harold checked that the rest of the group were all settled with a drink, took a large swig of his own porter, then raised his voice. "You lot! Listen up a minute. Thank you for all your hard work, first of all. We've all been thrust into positions that we never thought we'd even get near to, and with the military emergency we're having to find our feet really quickly. I really appreciate the enormous amount of effort and the long hours that everyone has been putting in."

"Hear, hear!" Rob, as vice president of the party, clearly felt compelled to second Harold's words.

"Shut up, Rob," Kim groaned. "I've been hearing that bloody phrase all day. If I hear it one more time I'm going to scream!" A few people chuckled, and Harold waited for the laughter to die down before continuing.

"As you all know, to speed this emergency bill up we introduced draft versions of it to both Houses at the same time. The Commons approved our version today, thank goodness, so that's the version that the Lords will be reading tomorrow at committee stage. Which reminds me that we need to withdraw the other one." Harold patted his pockets until he found a pen, grabbed a napkin from his table and tried to scribble a reminder on it, but the nib just broke the thin paper, the ink refusing to flow. "Shit!" Harold muttered, loud enough for Joanna to hear.

"It's okay, Harold," she soothed, patting his arm again. "Withdraw the draft Lords bill. On it."

"Thanks, Joanna." Harold took a moment to blow out a sigh and take another sip of his beer, while the rest of his Cabinet eyed him with concern. "Sorry, everybody – it's been a long few days, as you all know. Right – the emergency bill. Who have I put in the Foreign Office again?"

"Me, Harold." Naomi sounded like she was speaking to a spooked horse.

"Sorry." Another swig of porter. "Naomi, the Queen informed MI6 about the letter from Venezuela on Sunday, as soon as she learned about it from Prince Alexander. They called me yesterday morning and said that they are looking into it as a matter of extreme urgency, trying to find out if the Queen and the Prince of Wales are right to think that we might be facing a DF-41. Have you spoken to them? MI6, I mean."

"Yes, Harold, don't worry. I'm up to speed. They're still investigating."

"Okay. Thanks, Naomi. Thanks, everyone. Let's keep

up the hard work. The Queen chose this party to lead the country, so let's make Her Majesty proud."

Harold slumped back down into his chair to a murmur of "hear, hear" from Rhys and Joanna and a theatrical groan from Kim. Just as he was settling down to enjoy the rest of his pint, he felt a tap on his shoulder, and a voice close to his ear murmured "Prime Minister?"

"What?" Harold snapped, turning his head to see who the intruder was. He was faced with a young man, no older than thirty or so, wearing an immaculately tailored suit and a hurt expression. "Sorry," Harold added more gently. "Long day. What can I do for you?"

"I'm glad I found you, Prime Minister," the young man replied in a harried tone, slightly out of breath. "You weren't answering your phone."

"Oh." Harold extracted his phone from a pocket and glanced at the screen. "I'm sorry, I left it on silent. What is it?"

"My name is Matthew Arnot, sir. I work in the Speaker's Office. Dame Margaret herself sent me - she thought you'd want to see this."

"See what?"

"You'll need to come with me, I'm afraid."

"Fine." Harold drained the last of his beer and stood. "But unless the House is burning down again, our esteemed Madam Speaker owes me a drink."

* * *

"What do we want?"

"Justice!"

"When do we want it?"

"Now!"

"What do we—"

"Alice!"

Still shouting into her megaphone, which was kept handy in the SOAS Students' Union office for occasions like this one, Alice turned around to see who had called her name. "Hey, Cora!" she said in-between shouts. "Nice turnout, isn't it?"

"Yeah. Better than I was expecting. Must be at least fifty people here. That'll show this Stone guy, whoever he is. Right, Matilda?" Cora was addressing a young, pale-looking woman in glasses who was standing close behind her, a stack of slightly crumpled leaflets in one hand. She had wavy chestnut hair cut in a long bob, which suited her round face and high cheekbones. Alice thought she looked lovely, and slightly lost.

"Hi." Alice passed the megaphone over to Eda with a grateful smile and extended her hand. "I'm Alice, from SOAS. I don't think I've seen you around."

"No, I'm new. Matilda." The young woman gave Alice's hand a limp shake. "I only joined Students for Real Democracy a few months ago."

"Good! We always need new people."

"Especially since Alice here is off to become a big-shot lawyer," Cora added, elbowing Alice lightly in the ribs.

"Oh, really?" Matilda's big brown eyes widened. "That's so cool! I'm studying Law too, at UCL. I'm only in my first year, though."

"Enjoy it! Remember not to work too hard," Alice said with a wink which made Matilda's pale cheeks flush. "Oh, and if you're after textbooks for next year I'm selling mine, if you want to come and have a look."

"Sure, thanks!"

Eda had managed to get the crowd shouting "Hey-hey! Ho-ho! Harold Stone has to go!" on repeat, and Alice realised that making conversation was getting harder. "What's your Instagram?" she shouted over the noise.

Matilda bit her lip. "I don't have one, sorry."

Alice noticed the timid expression on Matilda's face and thought back to her own first year, when she had also been a little awestruck by third-year students. "That's okay!" she said, with what she hoped was a reassuring smile. "Do you have Twitter? Facebook? WhatsApp?"

Matilda shook her head, then fished her phone out of her pocket and handed it to Alice. "Can you just save your number? I'll ring you so you have mine."

"Sure." Alice waited for her phone to buzz and made sure to save Matilda's number. "There. Matilda, UCL. All done."

As she handed the phone back, Alice looked up and was surprised to see Big Ben looming over them to their left. "Finally! We're nearly there. Demos are always so slow! Especially when we haven't had time to get a permit and we have to pretend that we all just happened to go for a bloody stroll at the same time."

She looked around, realised that she couldn't recognise most of the people around her, then flashed another smile at Matilda and Cora. "Sorry, I'd better find the SOAS bloc again. Eda and I are both making speeches once we get to Westminster Bridge. If we don't get arrested first," she added, eyeing the handful of police officers on horseback which lined Parliament Square. "Wish me luck!"

Just then, the samba band started playing.

"There they are!" Alice waved and set off as quickly as she could towards the sound of the drums. On the way, her phone rang with a call from Fran.

"I'm here!" Fran panted. "I'm in front of the little Tesco's by Westminster Tube station. I can see a church opposite me – is that Westminster Abbey?"

"Oh, yeah, I know where you are," Alice reassured her. "Stay there. I'll come and find you."

When Alice and her friends were organising the protests, she had remembered that Fran worked at a department store on Oxford Street and had convinced her to come and join the protests for twenty minutes or so at the end of her shift, before racing back to Hackney to pick up her children from nursery.

"It's a complete attack on democracy," Alice had told her. "Who knows what these crackers are going to do to childcare provision? They seem all about pulling yourself up by your bootstraps and all that. They're probably bloody Thatcherites."

It was that last sentence – and her children's nursery being open until six – that had convinced Fran, whose first memory was of being carried on her dad's shoulder at a poll tax protest when she was three, to make the detour to Westminster.

"I feel young again," Fran told Alice once they had found each other and joined the SOAS bloc, where the samba band were putting on one of their best performances of the year. "I remember going to protests against the war in Iraq when I was in college. I was so full of anger and energy and hope back then. I haven't done this kind of thing in years."

"You *are* young, though," Alice observed, looking at her neighbour's still youthful face. Sure, a couple of lines were starting to appear around her mouth, and some grey hairs peppered her blonde ponytail, but who didn't have a few grey hairs after popping out two children and looking after them almost single-handedly? "What are you, thirty-five or something?" Alice asked.

"Thirty-four. I guess technically I *am* still quite young. If forty is the new thirty, then thirty must be the new twenty, right?"

"Exactly! You're basically my age."

"It doesn't feel that way, though," Fran continued with a sigh. "Between work and the kids, by the time they go to bed I just want to collapse on the sofa and watch Netflix. I haven't gone out at night in I don't even know how long. And the worst bit is that I don't even know if I'd want to anymore."

"Well, nightlife isn't for everyone," Alice observed. "I like going out and partying sometimes, but I definitely don't do it every weekend like the stereotypical student. But your anger, though – you said that when you were in college and protesting the war in Iraq you were full of anger. Aren't you angry still? About everything? The climate emergency, welfare cuts, poverty, all of that?"

"Yes, I am." Fran didn't seem to need to think about that. "It's not that my anger has gone away. But my energy has. When I hear about all those things that you just mentioned, I *do* get angry, but I'm so exhausted all the time that I don't even have the bandwidth to think about what I could do to help change things. You inspire me, though – you're always organising protests and things like that. I don't know how you keep it up."

"I haven't got two young children to feed and take care of, though. It's just me. Women have been told for decades that we can have it all, so now we're supposed to just *do it* all by ourselves, and if we can't cope it's on us. I swear, the feminist struggle has taken a very wrong turn."

Fran glanced at her phone. "Speaking of all that, I've got to go in ten minutes. Let me make the most of this protest."

At that moment, the samba band stopped playing and Emery swapped their sitar for a megaphone. "What do we want?" they called.

"Justice!" Fran yelled at the top of her voice. Alice saw anger in her eyes, but a flicker of hope, too.

* * *

When a footman knocked on the door and entered the room bearing a phone and an apologetic look, Queen Isabel had just stepped out of a long, hot bath and was preparing for bed.

"The Prime Minister, Your Majesty," the footman murmured. "He insisted it was urgent."

The Queen grabbed the phone with a scowl deep enough to send the footman scurrying away. "There had better be a constitutional crisis, Prime Minister," she snapped into the receiver.

Mr Stone's tone was as apologetic as the footman's expression had been. "I'm so sorry to disturb you at this hour, Your Majesty. It's not a constitutional crisis, but there's a crowd of protesters right outside the Houses of Parliament. There's got to be at least a hundred of them. They have a marching band, too."

Isabel waited for the Prime Minister to continue his

sentence and was surprised when it became clear that he had stopped talking. "And?" she prompted. "What is your point, Mr Stone?"

"Well ... This wasn't planned, ma'am. At least, nobody told *me* about it. I don't even know if they have permission to be holding a protest."

Was that fear in the Prime Minister's voice? Isabel supposed she ought to feel sorry for the man – after all, she had thrust him into a position for which he had clearly not been preparing. But to call her late at night because of a handful of layabouts was simply ridiculous.

"Look, Mr Stone," she barked into the phone, "it's just a bunch of protesters. There are always going to be protesters. If you want them cleared out, I suggest you contact the Metropolitan Police. Good night, Prime Minister."

Isabel put the phone down on a sideboard and started to remove her makeup. Not two minutes later there was another knock on her door. "What now?" she shouted.

The same footman inched his way into the room. "I'm so sorry, Your Majesty," he said with a bow, "but the Ravenmaster is here. He said—"

"Let me guess. He said it was urgent."

"Well, y-yes, ma'am, he did."

"Unbelievable." Isabel rolled her eyes. "Tell him to meet me in my study, five minutes." The Queen looked at herself in the mirror and considered whether to put makeup on for the second time that day but decided against it. Why should she bother? If Maloney was going to show up at this hour, he could put up with the sight of her wrinkles. A housecoat and a loose skirt thrown on over her nightgown would do. Besides, the man was the picture of deference, and hardly ever looked at her directly.

As predicted, the Ravenmaster kept his eyes lowered even after his bow. Isabel studied the bald patch on his head and decided that she had seen quite enough of it in the past few days.

"Mr Maloney," she said coolly, "I'm sure you won't be surprised to hear that I don't normally receive visitors at this hour. What's the matter now? This can't be about another raven, surely?"

The Ravenmaster flinched. "It is, Your Majesty," he rasped, as if struggling to find enough voice to speak. "Connie has been gone for twenty-four hours now. I think she left while I was telling Your Majesty about Ness. And the Resident Governor has asked me to inform Your Majesty that another crack has been discovered, at the top of the north-west corner of the White Tower." The Ravenmaster was clearly running out of steam, and the last part of his sentence came out in a whisper.

The Queen thought back to a visit to the Tower of London, when she had been told that the job of Ravenmaster could only be held by someone who had achieved officer-level rank in one of the armed forces. How could Maloney have managed that, if the mere sight of his Queen turned him into a quivering wreck?

"You should know, Mr Maloney," Isabel warned, "that this is the second time in ten minutes that I have been summoned by an inept man." The Ravenmaster flinched again but did not interrupt. "I can see that I am going to have to take matters into my own hands. Is there someone I can speak to about these ravens, and what might be causing them to leave?"

Maloney pursed his lips. "We use the vets at London Zoo, ma'am."

"Fine." The Queen picked up the phone on her desk, pressed a button and waited until a sleep-addled Cecilia picked up. "Cecilia, cancel my engagements for tomorrow morning. I'm going to the zoo."

Replacing the phone in its cradle and leaving a baffled Cecilia to deal with clearing her schedule, Isabel turned back to the Ravenmaster. "As for the cracks in the Tower, tell the Resident Governor to get some blasted cement, or whatever it is that's needed. Either that, or she can pack her bags, and I'm sure we can find a replacement."

"Yes, ma'am." The Ravenmaster bowed his head but did not leave.

"Was there anything else, Mr Maloney? I was hoping to be in bed by now."

"Just one more thing, ma'am. With so many of the ravens gone ... does Your Majesty think it's time to let the public know?"

Isabel thought of the protests outside Parliament. "No," she decided. "Nobody needs to know. Now, if you'll excuse me, I'm going to sleep. I can't believe I'm saying this, but I'll see you tomorrow morning, nine o'clock, at London Zoo."

* * *

"What did the Queen say, Harold?" Naomi put a hand on Harold's arm. The contact made Harold realise how tightly he was gripping the terrace rail, and he tried to relax his grip.

"She ignored me. Told me off like I was a schoolboy

and said to call the police if I wanted the rabble cleared out. Made me feel like I was back at bloody military school, the way she dismissed me."

"It's okay. We'll figure it out."

Harold stared down into the murky waters of the Thames. From Westminster Bridge, only a stone's throw away, came the tinny sound of a speech being delivered through a megaphone. Harold couldn't make out every word, but he heard enough to get the gist:

"Resign now!"

"Undemocratic!"

"Disgrace!"

With a sigh, Harold turned towards those Cabinet members who had still been at the pub with him when the protest had started. "Where's Rob?"

"He's on his way, Harold," Rhys replied. "He just went to meet his wife at the Strangers' Bar. He said he's rushing back."

Harold nodded solemnly and decided that he should probably call his own wife at some point. She might have some good advice to offer, too – Mavis had always been the level-headed one in their relationship.

Harold was just about to call her when Rob appeared at a jog. "I'm here!" he panted. "What's up?"

"That." Harold motioned with his head towards the bridge. "What are we going to do about them?"

"I don't know." Rob shrugged. "Why are you asking me?" Steve gave a snort, and Rob frowned. "Oh, wait – it's because I'm the Home Secretary now, isn't it?"

"Yes, Rob." Harold ran his hand through his thin pate of hair. "What are we going to do about these protesters, Mr Home Secretary?"

"I have no idea, Mr Prime Minister." Rob glanced towards the bridge. "Do we have to do anything? I mean, they're making a lot of noise, but they don't seem to be doing much else. And this is hardly a residential area, unless you count the Speakers. No offence, Dame Margaret," he added, turning to the Speaker of the House of Commons.

"None taken," Dame Margaret replied evenly. "So, Prime Minister, have you made a decision?"

"I don't know." Harold leaned on the railing, feeling the full weight of his sixty-three years bearing down upon him. "You've been in Parliament twice as long as I have, Dame Margaret. What do you think I should do?"

The Speaker took a moment before replying. "Well, protesters are always a headache. They're unpredictable. When a crowd is riled up, it doesn't take much to tip them over the edge into doing something stupid – just think of football.

"On the other hand, I think Mr Mbuko has a point. This group haven't done anything violent, just a lot of shouting and drumming. It might be wiser to let them be, at least for the moment. Parliament is protected, anyway, and I'm sure the police will intervene if things get out of hand. But in my experience folks get just tired and go home, ninety percent of the time," she remarked.

"Okay." Harold ran his fingers through his hair again. "So you'd feel safe enough if we waited to see what happens?"

"Yes. Don't worry about me. I called you over because I thought you should know what was going on, but I'm not concerned. This is Britain, Mr Stone – protests don't last."

Harold looked around at his Cabinet and saw from

their relieved faces that Dame Margaret's words had convinced them too. "Okay," he said again. "Rob, do me a favour and ask the police to be on the alert but to leave the protesters alone unless they start up something dodgy."

"Yes, boss. Is it alright if I go back to the Strangers' Bar after that? I'm sure Sharon's finished her Martini by now. I need to catch up!"

As if on cue, Harold's phone pinged with a text from his own wife: *Where are you? It's late*.

"Fine, but I don't know how you have the energy to go back to the bar." Harold stifled a yawn. "I'm going to bed. Call me if Parliament falls."

WEDNESDAY

Isabel decided to get straight to the point. "So, Dr Simco, do you have any conjectures as to why we are losing all these ravens all of a sudden?"

Dr Helen Simco looked more prepared for a day of plumbing than for an audience with the Queen. She was wearing muddy trainers, jeans with faded patches on the knees and a grey hoodie which was fraying at the edges.

When the Ravenmaster had ushered the Queen inside Helen's tiny office at the zoo and introduced them, the resident avian vet had had to whip off her rubber gloves and baseball cap before bobbing a curtsy. Isabel tried to imagine her delivering the weekly lecture she was apparently contracted for at the London School of Hygiene and Tropical Medicine, wearing a pink skirt suit, perhaps, with some tasselled patent leather loafers. It required quite a stretch of the imagination.

"I'm not sure, Your Majesty," Dr Simco replied after a few moments. "There could be a number of reasons. It's hard to tell without examining the ravens' habitat."

"I take it Mr Maloney has not asked you to do that?"

Isabel saw a look pass between the vet and the Ravenmaster, and Maloney cleared his throat. The Queen held up a hand to silence him. "I'm asking Dr Simco, Mr Maloney."

The Ravenmaster bowed his head, his lips thinly stretched, as if he had eaten a sour grape and was trying to keep a straight face.

"He hasn't asked me this time, ma'am," Dr Simco replied. "But, of course, I have visited the Tower many times, when one of the ravens has been unwell. There was nothing in their habitat on any of those visits to suggest that they might want to leave. They had plenty of good nourishment and a stimulating environment. Unless something's changed, I don't see why this should be happening."

This time, Isabel turned to the Ravenmaster. "*Has* anything changed, Mr Maloney?"

The Ravenmaster shook his head. "I'm not a vet myself, of course, Your Majesty, but I haven't deliberately changed anything in the ravens' environment or routine, nor have any of my assistants. And the birds which have left seem to have done so at different times in the day, and quite possibly from different places. I'm afraid to say that I'm stumped, ma'am."

"Yes, I'd figured as much." The Ravenmaster flinched and pursed his lips before giving another slight bow, and Isabel realised that her comment had cut deep. But her patience was wearing thin, and she had much more important things to be doing than sit in a cupboard-sized office in a zoo talking with a woman who stank of guano. "Dr Simco, would you be available to visit the Tower now?" she decided to ask.

Dr Simco frowned, but only for a moment. "Yes, of course, Your Majesty," she replied swiftly. "I'll just need to inform the general manager. Just give me two minutes, please, ma'am."

* * *

Half an hour later, the Queen, the Ravenmaster and Dr Simco stepped out of the royal car at the entrance to the

Tower of London and were met by a surprised and harried-looking Resident Governor, who had been phoned en route by Mr Maloney and told to clear the Tower of all visitors.

The Governor, Colonel Mary Burgess, bent herself double with offers of refreshments and visits to the Crown jewels, but Isabel walked briskly past the scores of Yeoman Warders who were standing to attention in front of the moat and ordered the Ravenmaster to lead their little group to the ravens' enclosure.

While Dr Simco examined the room and was briefed by one of Maloney's assistants on the content and frequency of the birds' meals, the Ravenmaster explained the ravens' living arrangements to the Queen. "I believe I have done everything by the book, Your Majesty," he said with a mournful shake of his head. "The enclosure is fox-proof, but the birds can't hurt themselves on the fence because the wire bends if they hit it. I give them plenty of food and follow a diet that Dr Simco drew up for me. I trim their flight feathers so they can't go too far. I just don't know where I went wrong."

Once Dr Simco had studied the ravens' enclosure and ascertained that there were no signs of a fox break-in, she asked Maloney to accompany her on a tour of the Tower grounds so she could identify any hazards to the birds and give the remaining ravens a medical examination. Isabel took the opportunity to ask for Colonel Burgess and enquire about the cracks in the White Tower.

"I was just showing them to Mr Steele, Your Majesty," said the Resident Governor, leading the Queen through the grounds until they stood facing what Colonel Burgess explained was the southeastern corner of the White Tower. "He specialises in the restoration of medieval buildings.

He's taking a look now."

The Governor pointed at a figure dressed in a hi-vis jacket and a hard hat, who was climbing a scaffold. Isabel raised her gaze past him and spotted a large crack in the domed roof. "That's the first crack we noticed – up there on the dome. That's the apse of the chapel. And the other one is round here." Colonel Burgess led Isabel round to the opposite side of the building. "It's right there, ma'am," she said, pointing to the top of a square tower, where a large crack could be seen running from the top of the tower to a small window halfway down.

"That's odd," the Governor added, squinting and shading her eyes with one hand. "It looked smaller yesterday. Perhaps I need to go to Specsavers again!" she said with a nervous laugh.

Isabel studied the crack, which did indeed look big – almost as big as the one on the roof of the chapel. "How is this possible?" she asked. "I mean, they are all individual stones, by the looks of it. How can so many of them crack at once?"

"I don't know, ma'am." Colonel Burgess shook her head. "I'm afraid we'll have to wait and see what Mr Steele and his team have to say. But I can assure Your Majesty that the cracks will be repaired. This building has guarded London for nearly a thousand years, and it won't fall to pieces on my watch."

"Good to know. I don't want the White Tower to go the way the ravens are going. Speaking of which, let's find Dr Simco and Mr Maloney. I don't have all day."

Dr Simco had just finished her inspection of the Tower. Isabel finally accepted the Governor's offer of tea and asked her to fetch Mr Steele, so both experts could make their reports.

"I haven't yet examined the crack on the northwestern corner, Your Majesty," said Mr Steele, "but I can't think why there should be a crack on the chapel apse. The rest of the roof is in good condition, and Colonel Burgess tells me that nothing has struck the building. I'll have another look, of course, but I just can't imagine where that crack came from."

"Can it be repaired, at least?" Isabel asked.

"Oh, yes, ma'am. It'll be a huge job, though. It's a mighty big crack, and you always have to be careful with a building this old. I can do it, though. It will just take a while."

"Fine. And what about the ravens, Dr Simco?"

The vet exchanged a pained look with the Ravenmaster. "I'm afraid I have to agree with Mr Maloney, Your Majesty. There is no apparent reason why the ravens should be leaving. Their environment is safe, they have plenty of space and food, and the three ravens that remain are all healthy. I have no idea what drove the other birds away – it's a mystery."

"Right." Isabel put down her half-empty cup of tea and stood up. "Well, let's just hope that it's all a silly legend, then. Now, if you'll excuse me, I need to get back to work."

* * *

Harold stared at the pile of papers in his despatch box and tried not to despair. He definitely needed to hire more staff – the Downing Street folks were great, but they were used to incoming Prime Ministers bringing their own retinue of acolytes to swell the ranks. Everyone was stretched to their limit, and although the ministers and staff kept a brave face and a smile on for Harold, the dark circles under their eyes spoke volumes. At least the protests of the night before had resolved into nothing – Dame Margaret had been right.

Harold was just about to pick up the phone and ask Steve to recommend a political secretary for him when the receiver rang under his hand. It was Tom, one of the receptionists. "Mr Haycroft is here to see you, Prime Minister," he murmured into the phone.

Harold frowned in concentration as he tried to place the name. "I'm sorry, who?"

"Maxwell Haycroft, sir." Tom's voice had dropped even lower and was now a whisper which Harold had to strain to decipher. "The head of MI6."

"Oh." Harold scanned his over-scribbled Filofax and made a mental note to ask Tom to set up a Google Calendar account. "Did I forget an appointment with him?"

"No, Prime Minister, but Mr Haycroft insists that he should speak with you as a matter of urgency."

"Oh." Harold resisted the urge to shout "*What now?*" down the phone. Instead, he pursed his lips and took a slow breath through his nose. "Of course. Send him in."

Maxwell Haycroft was an imposingly tall man, with intense grey eyes – almost the same shade as his hair – which made him seem like he was searching inside you for nasty little secrets. His impeccable black suit looked fresh from the tailor, and Harold – who had a penchant for brown tweed and had not had time to get the fraying cuffs of his jacket repaired – jumped up from his chair at the sight of Haycroft and had to resist the urge to salute, despite having studiously avoided active military duty for nearly forty years.

"Prime Minister." Haycroft dipped his head a fraction as he gave Harold's hand a firm shake. "Excuse me for coming over unannounced, but I thought the matter would be best discussed in person."

"But of course, of course." Harold pointed to the chair on the other side of his desk and waited for Haycroft to lower himself into it before resuming his own seat. "I'm sorry I haven't had a chance to visit your offices yet, Mr Haycroft. As you can imagine, I've been extremely busy."

"Yes, well, so have we." Haycroft glanced all around Harold's office before placing a slim briefcase on the desk. "Prime Minister, what I'm about to tell you is extremely confidential, as things usually are in my line of business – and indeed in yours. I don't mean to be impertinent, but can I trust that this room is free from interference?"

Harold ran a hand through his hair. "I mean, it's the Prime Minister's office. I presume it's secure."

The way Haycroft raised an eyebrow reminded Harold of a particularly nasty History teacher he'd had at senior school, who would spend the last ten minutes of every lesson testing his pupils and seemed to take it as a personal offence when someone gave the wrong answer.

"I don't have any reason to suspect that I'm being spied on," Harold added quickly. "Though I've obviously only been here for a few days."

"You haven't noticed any strange objects in the room? Any unexpected sounds when you're on the phone?"

"Not unless you count my dog!" Harold laughed. "She always seems to start barking when I'm on the phone with my wife. We joke that she's saying hello."

Haycroft did not laugh along, but simply nodded. "Alright." He opened his briefcase and pulled out a thick stack of papers. Harold noted the large red letters spelling *CONFIDENTIAL* across the top sheet.

"This is a report from my agents in Venezuela." Haycroft slid a file across the desk to Harold. "This one is from Singapore. And this one is from some MI5 agents here in London."

Harold opened the files and scanned their cover sheets. A few repeated words jumped out from all three: 'Bolivarian Government of Venezuela', 'PetrIsland Corp.', 'DF-41', 'HRH Prince Alexander'.

"Already?" Harold frowned. "But it's only been a few days. You reckon you've got to the bottom of this so quickly?"

"We have good connections in Venezuela. Things haven't been great for a while over there, economically speaking. Information's not that hard to get, if you're prepared to pay the price." Had this been a 007 film, Haycroft might have winked at this point, or at least given Harold a sly grin, but the man remained stone-faced. "And I'm afraid to say that the Prince of Wales is not the most cautious of people when it comes to his privacy, or that of his company."

"Okay." Harold wrung his hands as he paused to reflect for a moment, trying to keep his adrenaline at bay. "So, give it to me straight. Are we about to be attacked by a DF-41? Do we need to evacuate the whole of Cornwall? How much time have we got?"

Harold was expecting Haycroft to launch into a rushed timeline, but the head of MI6 merely raised an eyebrow again. "There will be no attack, Prime Minister."

"Oh?" Harold felt his heart rate slow down and let out a sigh of relief. "Our sanctions worked, then! I knew they would. Especially with the US on our side. Although this means that my term in government is over already. Oh, well. I'd better start—"

"Prime Minister." Haycroft silenced Harold with a raised hand. "There will be no attack because there are no missiles. Nor does the Venezuelan government have any reason to desire a conflict with us."

"But ... but their letter to Prince Alexander made it very clear that they intended to attack. Unless His Royal Highness's company stopped cartel trading, but they were never doing that, were they? The whole thing was made up!"

"Exactly, Prime Minister." Haycroft's expression, which had been serious to begin with, became positively grave. "The whole thing was made up. Not just the cartel. I'm afraid you'll find evidence in these files that the letter was fabricated by the Prince of Wales. It wasn't posted in Caracas - someone stuck a fake Venezuelan postmark and stamp on the envelope and snuck it inside a post office in a village near Truro."

"What?" Harold's adrenaline levels surged again. "But why would the Prince of Wales do such a thing?"

Haycroft smiled for the first time since he had entered Harold's office, but it was a smile full of pity. "You'll have to ask him that question yourself, Prime Minister. And for that, sir, you have my utmost sympathy."

* * *

For all the headaches and sleepless nights it caused, being Prime Minister certainly meant being able to get things done quickly when necessary. Within two hours of Haycroft's visit, Harold was on a government plane bound for Truro Airfield.

As he looked out of the small window at the rapidly disappearing silhouette of London City airport, Harold realised that he was wringing his hands harder than ever and started to regret flying alone but for the burly Downing Street police officer, who had remained professionally resistant to conversation throughout their drive to the airport.

But Harold needed Prince Alexander to tell him the truth about the Venezuelan business, and he had reasoned that a one-to-one would probably prove more effective than dropping in unannounced flanked by several Cabinet members. So, he took a deep breath, rolled his shoulders back and tried to focus on the *Telegraph* headlines.

The flight felt interminable to Harold, though in truth it probably only lasted an hour or so. A uniformed officer from the local police department was already at the airfield when Harold and his security guard landed, ready to drive them to Carrick Palace, Prince Alexander's residence.

Carrick Palace had been designed using an interesting mix of Neo-Gothic and Modernist architecture, and in regular circumstances Harold would have asked the driver to slow down so he could admire the view and take some pictures to show Mavis when he returned home. As it was, Harold barely noticed the high turrets and wide expanses of steel-framed glass. As soon as the car stopped and a footman opened his door, Harold bolted out – much to the chagrin of the two police officers accompanying him – and quickly followed the footman inside.

"Welcome, Prime Minister." The footman, dressed in a green livery bearing what Harold supposed must be the coat of arms of the Duchy of Cornwall, led the way through a glass-encased corridor and up a grand marble staircase. "His Royal Highness has been informed of your arrival and is expecting you in his study. I imagine you're familiar with the protocol?"

"Yes, yes." As he hurried up the stairs, past a series of seascapes in gilded frames, Harold thought about the previous Sunday, when he had shuffled nervously behind the Queen's equerry on his way to being made Prime Minister. How could only three days have passed since then?

Prince Alexander turned out to inspire much less awe in Harold than his mother the Queen. Harold had seen his picture plenty of times in the newspapers and on TV, but unlike most people the Prince of Wales somehow managed to look even younger in person than in the media. Though he was now in his mid-thirties, he still had the same fresh-faced, boyish look he'd sported at eighteen, when his arrival at Falmouth University had sent many of his fellow students into a frenzy.

Harold made his bow at the door before taking a couple of steps into the prince's study. It was a large corner room, brightly lit by two high windows and furnished with a mixture of antique pieces and sleek, contemporary focal points which reflected the architecture of the palace. As Harold entered the room, Prince Alexander rose from a low, nearly shapeless chair next to one of the windows and went to shake his hand.

"Hello, Prime Minister." The prince's greeting sounded slightly strained.

"Your Royal Highness, thank you for seeing me so quickly," Harold said with a polite smile.

"Well, you didn't give me much choice, did you?" Prince Alexander laughed nervously, and Harold wondered whether the prince suspected the reason for his visit. He followed his host to the seats by the window and proceeded to feel old as he struggled to lower himself into his chair – little more than a pouf, really – while the prince folded his youthful limbs into his own seat with effortless grace.

"I'm sorry to have come at such short notice, sir," Harold said once he had finally settled into the chair. "I wouldn't be imposing on Your Royal Highness's time if it weren't urgent."

"Well, then, get to the point, would you? I'm supposed to be meeting my friend Eric Blythe for a tennis match in half an hour."

"Of course, sir. Would Your Royal Highness kindly explain this?" Harold extracted the MI5 file from his briefcase and placed it on the low coffee table between them, open at the section detailing how the 'Venezuelan' letter was actually a Cornish fabrication.

"Wh-What is this?" Prince Alexander stuttered in fake confusion as Harold watched his eyes widen.

"I think Your Royal Highness knows very well what it is." Harold surprised himself with his own boldness, and mentally gave thanks that the Prince had returned to Cornwall so soon. Though it would have been quicker to meet him at Buckingham Palace, Harold was glad to have caught him alone. Confronting a thirty-five-year-old who looked no older than twenty was one thing; confronting his mother would be quite a different challenge.

"Excuse me?" Prince Alexander rasped. "Who do you think you are to talk to me like that?" Under his golden tan, Harold could detect a deep blush colouring the prince's cheeks.

"Forgive me, Your Royal Highness – I meant no disrespect." Harold knew that it would be no use antagonising the prince if he wanted to get to the bottom of the matter. He waited for Prince Alexander to give a mollified nod before continuing. "I have nothing but the interests of our great country at heart—"

"And those of the Crown, I hope?" the prince interjected with a smirk.

"Indeed, sir. And although I was a latecomer to politics, I have never had reason to think the interests of the Crown in conflict with those of the country."

This time, Prince Alexander's eyes narrowed like those of a cat preparing to fight. "And you think that has now changed?"

"That's not what I'm saying, sir."

"Then what *are* you saying, Prime Minister?"

"I just need Your Royal Highness to help me understand what happened here, please." Harold gestured at the file. "As far as I can make out, last Sunday Your Royal Highness informed Her Majesty the Queen that a letter had arrived from the Venezuelan government threatening military action because of something that Your Royal Highness's company hasn't actually done. Your Royal Highness also suspected that the Venezuelan armed forces might have one of the most powerful and farthest-reaching missiles in the world at their disposal. Have I got the story right so far, sir?"

"Yes." The prince sounded defiant.

"Great. So, Her Majesty plucked me out of obscurity and asked me to form a government because of my expertise in missiles and ballistics. And my government—"

"*Her Majesty's* government, Prime Minister," Prince Alexander interrupted with another smirk.

"I beg your pardon, sir. Of course. Her Majesty's government, which I have the undeserved privilege of leading, placed an emergency bill before Parliament. That bill, and an analogous one which our American colleagues approved yesterday, put in place economic sanctions aimed at discouraging the Venezuelan government from carrying out what we believed to be an unprovoked attack based on a lie.

"Now, this is where things get confusing for me, sir, so I would appreciate Your Royal Highness's help. The MI6 file from Singapore confirms that there is no evidence of PetrIsland Corp. or any other local refineries engaging in illicit cartels."

"Quite right."

"And if that were all, sir, I would have thought that it confirmed what we already knew, namely the fact that the Venezuelan government had made up an excuse to attack us with their missiles for some unfathomable reason. However, not only did the MI6 agents in Venezuela find no evidence of any missiles, they also found no evidence of the letter originating there. Apparently, it was posted here in Cornwall. Which brings me back to asking Your Royal Highness what is going on."

Prince Alexander did not answer immediately, and Harold could almost see the cogs turning in his brain, presumably trying to come up with a suitable explanation. In the end he settled on, "How should I know? Maybe this is someone's idea of a joke. Probably one of my staff."

"I see."

A few seconds of silence stretched between them, then Prince Alexander glanced at the clock above the door. "Was there anything else, Prime Minister? There's a tennis court with my name on it."

"Just one more thing, sir, if you please. Will Your Royal Highness be informing Her Majesty of the developments, or should I?"

A panicked look stole across the Prince's face. "My mother? What does she have to do with anything?"

"Well, obviously the emergency sanctions bill needed royal assent to become law. I imagine the Queen would be very surprised if Parliament sent over another emergency bill removing those sanctions in the space of a couple of days. I'd better let Her Majesty know in advance what's going on."

"But why would you want to cancel the sanctions, Prime Minister?"

Harold raised his eyebrows. "Because there is no reason to keep them in place, sir. We'll have to issue a formal apology to the Venezuelan government, too, now I think of it." Prince Alexander's face paled, and Harold continued: "Or is there something I don't know, Your Royal Highness?"

Prince Alexander emitted a deflated sigh. "Let me text Blythe. I think I'm going to have to cancel our tennis match. Can I hitch a lift on your plane?"

Harold exulted inside. "I would be most honoured of Your Royal Highness's company."

* * *

"Let me get this straight. You made the whole thing up?" Isabel stood up from her armchair and started pacing up and down the intricate Afghan rug which covered the floor of her study. When her son failed to leave his seat, she shot him a sharp glance. "Have you lost your manners as well as your mind?"

Prince Alexander rose wearily. "Sorry. I was just thinking."

"What about? The fact that you're going to make your mother, your Queen, look like a complete idiot in front of her own government?"

"They don't have to know, Mum."

Isabel sat down again and locked eyes with her son. "The Prime Minister already knows, Alexander. I may have told him to keep quiet until I'd spoken to you, but very few things stay secret for any length of time in Westminster. You know that."

"It's okay. I fobbed him off."

"Oh, please!" the Queen scoffed with a roll of her eyes. "You really think he bought that nonsense about it being a prank from one of your staff? I thought you were smarter than that, Alexander. Eton really was wasted on you." Isabel knew that her comment would smart, but she was too angry to care. Her son had done stupid things before, but this was a whole new level from the schoolboy scrapes she'd had to dig him out of in the past.

Alexander dropped his gaze and slumped back down into his chair, his shoulders hunched forwards. "What do you want me to say?"

"At least tell me why you did it."

"We were losing money."

"Who's 'we'?"

"PetrIsland."

"Okay." Isabel felt her toes curl in her shoes and took a deep breath. "So, your company was losing money. And why is that?"

"Because the price of crude oil had gone sky-high. I've never seen prices like that before, Mum. It was ridiculous. We couldn't have stayed in business for much longer if the trend continued. I would have lost all my investments. I would have been ruined, Mum."

Isabel had never seen her son look so scared. He might have lied about the letter, but there was no doubt that he was telling the truth now. His eyes were wide, his jaw clenched, and Isabel gave an inward groan at the realisation that Alexander must have invested all his assets into this one company. What kind of an idiot did he have for a financial adviser? Did he even have a financial adviser at all?

"Okay." Isabel took a deep breath as she thought about what Alexander was saying. "So, you decided that the solution to the increased cost of crude oil would be to fake a military threat from Venezuela. I'm not sure I follow."

Alexander had the grace to look sheepish. "I knew that the government and Parliament would react the way they did. Unless they were suddenly filled with Marxists or something, but that's not very likely to happen, is it?"

"You knew they would react how, exactly?"

"With sanctions, of course. It's always sanctions, in the first instance. They wouldn't attack straight away, not with the threat of a powerful missile like that hanging over their heads."

"And that's just great for you, isn't it?" Isabel spat.

"Of course it is. The price of crude oil has gone down massively in the past twenty-four hours."

Isabel spent several seconds staring silently at her son. "You're unbelievable," she said eventually.

"I know." Alexander flashed her his special grin. "You love me, really."

"What does that have to do with anything?" Isabel rolled her eyes again, but she knew that Alexander had got under her skin. She was a tough, confident decision-maker, bred to lead, but the one thing she had never been able to resist was her son's grin. It was pathetic, really, but there was nothing she could do about it. "So, what do you expect me to do?" she asked.

Alexander shrugged. "Just keep things as they are now. If Parliament or the government try to remove the sanctions, find a way to stop them. You can do that, right?"

Isabel thought for a few seconds. "Yes, I think so."

"Bingo!" Alexander grinned again. "Now, would you like to play some tennis? I had to cancel a match with Blythe to come here."

"I can't." Isabel stood again and gave her son a light cuff round the head. "Find somebody else to play with. I've got to clean up your mess."

* * *

"Hey, Hal. I thought you'd be at Buckingham Palace still."

Harold took a long pull of his beer while Rob took off his jacket and settled into the chair opposite him, facing out towards the bar of the Sports and Social. Despite the name of the place, Harold had not been feeling very sociable when he'd come in, and had chosen to face the wall in an attempt to minimise conversation. Rob was his friend, though – and besides, with all the work that he and the rest of the Cabinet had put in during the past few days, Harold definitely owed him a drink.

"Hey, Rob. No, the Queen and Prince Alexander wanted to talk in private. I'm sorry I haven't been to the Chamber yet – thought I'd have a pint first. Speaking of, what are you drinking?"

"You know I'm a Guinness man, Hal. And don't worry – there was nothing major on the agenda today, anyway. Finally, a bit of a breather."

"Good. One Guinness coming up."

As Harold returned to their table with Rob's beer, plus a fresh one for himself, he felt his friend's eyes give him the once-over. "Are you okay, Hal?" Rob asked. "You look a bit grey."

"Yeah, I'm fine. Just knackered. I can't believe it's only four p.m. – it feels more like nine."

"Well, you did just fly to Cornwall and back. What was that all about, by the way?"

Harold stalled for time by taking another long sip of his drink. "I shouldn't really tell you," he replied eventually.

"Ah, it's like that, is it?" Rob laughed, but it sounded hollow. "Half a week as Prime Minister and you're already full of state secrets that you can't even share with your right-hand man?"

"It's not like that."

"Sure." It was Rob's turn to fall silent and concentrate on his pint. Harold suddenly felt guilty – after all, it had been Rob's idea that Harold should run for president of the party when the position had become vacant seven years previously. Harold thought Rob should put himself forward instead – he was younger, more gregarious and a more confident public speaker – but Rob and Sharon's son Dwayne had only just turned one, and Rob had needed to spend as much time at home as possible. Had the timing been different, it might have been Rob whom the Queen's secretary heard speak at the Enterprise Awards event the previous winter, and Harold might never have found himself in Downing Street.

"Okay, I'll tell you," he said after a couple of minutes. "Just don't tell anybody else yet, alright? I promised Her Majesty, and I don't like to break my word."

"Of course, Hal. You know I wouldn't do that."

"Yes, I know." Harold downed the rest of his pint. "So, it turns out that the letter from Venezuela was a hoax. It was posted in Cornwall."

"What?" Rob spluttered. "But we've just imposed sanctions against them! And so have the US!"

"I know." Harold shook his head. "I wanted to introduce another emergency bill immediately, to revoke them, but the Prince of Wales asked me to wait. He said he wanted to explain the situation to the Queen in person, and I couldn't really refuse, could I? I mean, she's his mother."

"I guess. So, what happens now?"

"I don't know." Harold shrugged. "They're talking right now, and I imagine the Queen will let me know when they're finished. If I haven't heard from her in an hour or so I'll call Buckingham Palace myself."

"So, Hal ..." Rob paused to take a fortifying sip of his Guinness. "Is this the end of our government, then? Are we going to be the shortest government in history?"

"I guess so. I'm going to have to resign, Rob. The Queen asked me to form a government because she was worried about the military threat from Venezuela, and I have some expertise in that field. It turns out that there *is* no threat. I can't justify staying on, can I? I'd never keep the confidence of Parliament, anyway."

"Oh, *shit*." Rob's eyes widened, and he brought a hand to his mouth.

"It's okay, Rob, really. We never expected—"

"No, Hal, I wasn't talking about that." Rob turned towards the door. "Guess who just walked right past our table, really close? Definitely close enough to hear us? And then practically ran out the door?"

"Crap." Harold stood up and looked to the door as well, though it was obviously too late. "Who?"

"Caroline Banerjee, that's who."

"Fuck." Harold sank back down into his chair. "The Queen is going to have my balls for dinner."

* * *

When Major Phillips announced that the Ravenmaster was seeking an immediate audience, Isabel had to fight the urge to fling her teacup at the wall. She had already seen Mr Maloney once today - surely that was enough. When had the job of a monarch become mostly about dealing with a bunch of birds?

"Send him in," Isabel told her equerry with an exasperated sigh.

Maloney must have known that his presence would be less than welcome, because he entered the Queen's study slowly, almost dragging his feet. His bright red uniform was at odds with his gloomy expression, and after his bow the Ravenmaster remained bent as much as his stiffly starched collar permitted, as usual.

"What is it now, Mr Maloney?" Isabel snapped. "No, don't tell me – one of the ravens took offence at Dr Simco poking around the place today and left."

From her seated position the Queen had an easy view of the Ravenmaster's face, even as he stooped; at hearing her words, Maloney cringed, his features squeezing themselves together as if he were about to cry. "Kit, Your Majesty," he replied, his voice low as if in mourning. "I couldn't find him when I put the other ravens in their enclosure for the night. It appears that no-one has seen him all day, not since Dr Simco examined him this morning."

"I was under the impression that you didn't worry until twenty-four hours had passed," the Queen observed.

"Forgive me, Your Majesty." Maloney cringed again and stooped further. Isabel, taking pity on him, invited him to sit and rang for some more tea. Once he had thanked her repeatedly for both the seat and the drink, Maloney finally continued: "Your Majesty is right. Normally I wouldn't be particularly concerned unless a bird had been missing for at least twenty-four hours. But we have lost so many ravens recently that I thought I should inform Your Majesty as soon as there were new developments."

"I suppose you're right." Isabel sighed again and took a sip of her tea, feeling her irritation deflate slightly. "Remind me, Mr Maloney, how many ravens are left now?"

"T-Two, Your Majesty." The Ravenmaster's voice

broke on the number, and he sounded as if he couldn't quite believe what he was having to say. "And I'm afraid that's not all, Your Majesty."

"Oh? Am I going to need something stronger than tea, Ravenmaster?"

The Ravenmaster dipped his head again. "Perhaps, ma'am. The Resident Governor wishes me to inform Your Majesty that part of the White Tower has now collapsed."

"Excuse me?" Isabel's voice had risen without her meaning it to, and Maloney flinched. "What do you mean?" the Queen added more softly. "I was at the Tower today. Mr Steele didn't mention anything about a possible collapse. What happened?"

"The roof caved in, Your Majesty. The chapel roof first, and then the rest. Thankfully, there was nobody inside. Mr Steele is examining the damage, but he said he has no idea how it could have happened."

"Unbelievable." Isabel felt a shudder run through her. "I hadn't realised the damage was that bad. I don't know about you, Mr Maloney, but I've had quite enough of inexplicable things happening."

"As have I, ma'am."

Queen and Ravenmaster sat together in silence, finishing their tea, Isabel twirling her ring around her finger with vigour.

"I'm sorry, Your Majesty," Maloney said after a few minutes.

Isabel studied the Ravenmaster's lined face. "What are you sorry for, Mr Maloney?"

"For failing in my duty to Your Majesty. I have only one job – to keep the ravens healthy and safe. And I am failing miserably."

"No, you're not." Isabel fought against her annoyance and gave the Ravenmaster a reassuring smile. "It's not your fault that all the ravens seem to be leaving. Dr Simco said so herself."

"Thank you, Your Majesty."

"Now, Ravenmaster, I've had a very long day. You'll have to excuse me." The Queen stood, responded to Maloney's bow with a nod of her head and went off to bed.

* * *

Isabel slept in a luxurious four-poster bed with canopy, curtains, bedspread and matching cushions made of heavy burgundy brocade. She woke early, worked hard and was never really off-duty, always being on-call in case of a crisis and being denied any respite from having to behave like the Queen she was.

Consequently, she considered herself entitled to the best sleep possible, and – with her nightly chamomile tea and her sumptuous bed – she usually achieved it. That night, however, she could not settle. For the best part of an hour, she tossed and turned, thinking of nothing in particular but unable to relax; only after ringing for a second cup of herbal tea did Isabel finally manage to fall asleep.

The Queen dreamt that she was back at the Tower of London. She entered the usual way and made her way past the moat and the Casemates, through the Outer Ward and then the Inner one, until she was in the centre of the complex and staring at the White Tower. Then, right in front of her eyes, the White

Tower started to crumble to the ground. First the roof caved in, then the walls came apart, stone falling upon stone, a great cloud of dust enveloping Isabel until she started to cough, tears streaming from her eyes.

The tears made it hard to see clearly, but as the last of what had been the White Tower tumbled away, Isabel could have sworn she saw a large black bird fly from the ruins, rise in a high arc over her head and disappear from sight. Somehow, with the logic that only applies in dreams, the Queen knew with absolute certainty that that had been the very last of the Tower's ravens.

Isabel woke up covered in sweat, her heart racing, and had to call a maid for a third cup of chamomile tea.

THURSDAY

Early the next morning, Harold made his way to Buckingham Palace in a dejected mood. He had known from the start that his government would be short, bound by a vote of confidence which had been given on the understanding that it would be revoked as soon as the military threat had been neutralised.

Harold felt genuinely grateful to have been given the opportunity to form a government at all, even if it was to be the shortest in British history - but he had hoped to resign with dignity. Instead, as he stared at the familiar buildings of Westminster filing past him on the short drive to the Queen's residence, Harold felt like a naughty schoolboy caught cheating on an exam, on his way to being punished by the headmaster.

As he walked through the hallways of Buckingham Palace and into the Queen's study, Harold felt a jolt in his stomach much like the one he had felt on his first visit, four interminable days earlier. This time, though, he tried to commit to memory as many of the paintings and other decorations which adorned the place as he could, not knowing whether he would ever see them again. Mavis deserved that much from him.

"Good morning, Prime Minister."

"Good morning, Your Majesty." Harold bowed, then tentatively made his way towards the Queen and shook her hand. "I apologise for bothering you so early, ma'am. I know it's been a very long week already."

"Not at all," the Queen said genially. Was that a smile on her lips? She was in a much better mood than Harold had expected, given Prince Alexander's revelations the previous day.

As soon as they were both seated, Harold decided to go straight to the point. "I won't take up much of your time, ma'am. I requested an audience because I would like to tender my resignation as Prime Minister of Your Majesty's government." Harold's voice quivered slightly as he added, "It's been an honour to serve you, Your Majesty."

The Queen did not reply immediately, but studied Harold's face for a few seconds, until he became uncomfortable and dropped his gaze. When she spoke, the Queen was brief: "I do not accept your resignation, Prime Minister."

"I beg your pardon, ma'am?" Harold was struggling to believe his ears. Even if the Queen didn't yet know that the Labour leader had overheard him talking about the fake letter, surely she understood that there was no reason for him to stay in government. What reason *could* there be for him to stay, now that the threat from Venezuela had turned out to be a hoax?

"I think you're being too hasty, Prime Minister," the Queen remarked with a rare smile. "I've been rather impressed by your performance so far. You managed to form a government, get Parliament on your side, pass a controversial piece of legislation and get our American friends to do the same, all inside of three days. That's impressive, coming from the leader of a tiny party. Wouldn't you agree?"

Harold thought for a few moments before replying. "Thank you, Your Majesty," he said eventually, dipping his head. "But I'm afraid that Parliament is not really on my side at all. They gave their vote of confidence on the strict understanding that it would be revoked as soon as Venezuela no longer posed a threat to us. I'm sure Your Majesty knows by now that they never posed a threat to begin with. His Royal Highness told Your Majesty the truth, did he not?"

"Ah, yes, that." The Queen's jovial expression clouded over for a moment, then immediately brightened up again. "My son has always been a little irresponsible, but that was a particularly stupid thing to do, even for him. Don't worry, Prime Minister – I've given him a stern talking-to. He won't do it again."

Harold didn't have any children of his own, but the way the Queen had just spoken about Prince Alexander reminded him of something his brother Craig might have said about his daughter Tilly when she was a toddler. It didn't sound like the way most people would talk about someone in their mid-thirties. But what could Harold do? It wasn't like he had any power to punish the Prince of Wales for his irresponsible behaviour. He might not like the guy, but Prince Alexander was the Queen's son and heir, and he was entitled to Harold's deference.

"Now, Prime Minister," the Queen continued, "my son might have gone about it in a very childish way, but it turns out that he was only trying to keep his company afloat. So, I need you to keep those sanctions in place, please."

"Ma'am?" The Queen had asked him to continue down a very rocky diplomatic path in the same tone Mavis might have used to ask him to pick up some milk on his way home. "But there's no justification for keeping the sanctions going, ma'am," Harold ventured. "The Venezuelan government hasn't threatened us at all."

"Well, Parliament don't need to be told that, do they? The power to impose sanctions rests with the government. Besides, I need a government in place to handle the diplomatic crisis which is now inevitable. I'm sure you already know that Russia has threatened to suspend all oil and gas imports to the UK to avenge their Venezuelan friends. We can't afford another power vacuum now."

Harold felt himself blush and dipped his head again, clasping his quivering hands in his lap. "It's not as simple as that, Your Majesty," he forced himself to admit. "I'm afraid I have been careless. I was telling Robert Mbuko about the fake letter, and I didn't realise that Ms Banerjee was nearby. I'm pretty sure that she heard us. She's bound to demand a vote of no confidence first thing today, and I'm sure the papers will have heard about it all by now, too. I'm sorry, ma'am." Harold bowed his head lower in shame, fixing his gaze on the swirly floral patterns in the plush beige carpet.

"I see." The Queen's expression darkened again.

That's it, Harold thought. *She's bound to accept my resignation now.* The Queen, however, simply clasped her hands in her lap, turning the ring on her right hand round and round. "That's fine, Prime Minister," she said after a few moments. "I mean, it's a nuisance, but it's nothing we can't deal with. Leave it to me."

Harold considered what the Queen might mean by 'nothing *we* can't deal with'. Was she using the royal 'we', or did she mean to include Harold? Or somebody else, perhaps? Prince Alexander?

Harold was about to ask for clarification when the Queen spoke again. "Prime Minister, what did you think of Mr Fivecoat, when he was in government?"

Once again, Harold was taken aback. What did Fivecoat have to do with the current situation? "I don't know, ma'am," he replied, trying to buy himself some thinking time with a non-committal answer. "I suppose I thought that he was very ... balanced. A real centrist."

"And what's your opinion of centrism, Mr Stone?"

The Queen's tone was even, and Harold couldn't see where she was going with these questions. "I'm not sure, ma'am," he said, once again wondering what the right answer would be. "I think centrism has a lot to recommend it, but it can also lead to paralysis. It can be hard to get anything done if one is too preoccupied with not tipping the scales either way. I guess sometimes a leader has to be decisive and commit to a course of action."

"Quite right," said the Queen, and Harold gave an inward smile of relief at having guessed the correct answer. "And are you a decisive leader, Mr Stone?"

Harold's relief was quickly replaced by dread. His heartbeat quickened and his neck and armpits started to sweat as his brain was flooded with images of the HMS Loxley burning. A name pulsed insistently in his mind: *Able Rate Geoffrey McNeal.*

"Are you alright, Mr Stone?" The Queen's concerned voice cut through Harold's thoughts, and he concentrated on taking a deep breath.

"I'm fine, ma'am," he rasped, his throat dry. "I apologise. And yes, Your Majesty," he compelled himself to add, "I *am* a decisive leader." A shiver ran through Harold's body as he forced out what he knew to be a lie.

The Queen studied him with a critical eye for a

moment but must have decided that he was telling the truth. "Good. As I was saying earlier, you have impressed me with your performance in government so far. I'll admit that I share your assessment of Mr Fivecoat and his politics. I believe that his brand of centrism might have been behind both his victory five years ago and his downfall since. A lot of voters seem to favour moderate leaders and then criticise them for not getting much done, don't you think?"

"Yes, ma'am." Harold had grabbed the opportunity to take a few more deep breaths while the Queen talked, and his heart rate was approaching normal again.

"Well, Mr Stone," the Queen concluded, "I think you might be exactly what this country needs. A decisive leader who gets things done."

"Thank you, ma'am, but—"

The Queen raised a hand to stop Harold in his tracks. "Mr Stone, as you said yourself, it's been a very long day. I suggest you get through today as best you can, and then go home early and have a nice dinner and a glass of wine with your wife. What was her name again?"

"Mavis, Your Majesty."

"Of course. Mavis. You must bring her to my garden party in a couple of weeks. Anyway, have a nice dinner with Mavis tonight and a good sleep. I'm sure tomorrow you'll wake up feeling refreshed, and you'll thank me for not accepting your resignation. Good day, Prime Minister."

The Queen rang the bell which signalled to the footmen that they should open the heavy double doors. Harold had no choice but to bow, murmur "Your Majesty" and retreat, dazed, back to his armoured government car.

* * *

"Do you like bluebells, Cecilia?"

The Queen's private secretary looked up with a frown from the papers she was organising. "Ma'am?"

"It's a simple question. Do you like bluebells?"

"Well, yes, ma'am. They're rather pretty, I think."

"I think so too." Isabel tapped a few keys on her computer before turning to look at Cecilia again. "Lady Gillian went to Kew Gardens for her granddaughter's birthday last weekend, and she was telling me that they have some glorious bluebells this time of year. Cherry blossoms, too. I was thinking that we could reward ourselves for how hard we've been working recently and have ourselves a little day trip."

"'We', ma'am?"

"Yes. You and I. We both deserve it, don't you think?"

"Oh." Cecilia paused in thought for a moment before adding quickly, "Thank you, Your Majesty. That would be very nice. And I'm sure everyone at the Gardens would be delighted with a royal visit."

"Quite. And while we're there we could pop into the National Archives, too, and have a look around. We might find something useful."

"Oh," Cecilia said again. Within a moment, understanding spread across her face – one doesn't rise to the post of private secretary to the Queen by the age of thirty-five without possessing a good dose of wits. "And is there any collection in particular that Your Majesty wishes to view? I might alert the archivists in advance, just in case any of the documents are stored off site."

"Tell them that I'd like to view the Crown records. I'm not

sure which departments, exactly, but definitely the Chancery. Nothing internal to the Royal Household – I'm interested in public-facing records. Legislative records."

"Yes, ma'am. And when would Your Majesty like to visit the Archives?"

"This afternoon, if possible. And ask them to find me a Constitutional Law expert, too."

Cecilia sat up with a jolt, but quickly recovered her composure. "Yes, ma'am. I'll inform the Gardens and the Archives and get a car ready. Shall I tell the Gardens staff that Your Majesty will be having lunch there?"

"Yes, please, and yourself, of course."

"Thank you, Your Majesty."

Cecilia gathered her papers, curtsied and was about to leave the room when the Queen called after her, "And, Cecilia ...?"

"Yes, ma'am?"

"I understand that I'll be descending upon these people at no notice, but please tell them not to go to too much trouble. I have many things to worry about, and the quality of the sandwiches at Kew Gardens is not one of them."

"Yes, Your Majesty." Cecilia curtsied again and left to make the necessary phone calls.

Isabel gave the tabs on her browser a final glance, then shut her computer down with a satisfying *click* and went to find her favourite waterproof shoes.

* * *

Less than half an hour later, Isabel and Cecilia were in a car bound for the Royal Botanic Gardens at Kew. Their visit was pleasant and uneventful: they walked among the bluebells and down the Cherry Walk, had a quick lunch of cucumber sandwiches and Victoria sponge with the flustered but obsequious director of the Gardens, then made their excuses and got back into the waiting car for the five-minute drive to the sleek glass-fronted building which houses the National Archives.

The Queen and her private secretary were met by Dr Pamela Boland, Head of Research, a diminutive lady wearing a tweed skirt, round metal-framed glasses and a shoulder-length bob of brown hair which made her look like such a stereotypical archivist that Isabel struggled not to laugh. Next to her was a pale, gaunt-faced man carrying a large leather suitcase, who introduced himself as Professor David Dunham, an expert in Constitutional Law from University College London.

"We're honoured that Your Majesty chose to visit us," Dr Boland said. "Though, of course, I would be more than happy to personally deliver any records that Your Majesty wanted to review in the future."

"Thank you, Dr Boland. My secretary and I were headed to the Botanical Gardens anyway, so I thought it would be a convenient time to pop in."

"Very well, ma'am. Would you like to follow me?"

Isabel, Cecilia and Dunham followed the archivist into one of the manuscript reading rooms, a dimly lit space sparsely furnished with worn wooden desks, hard-backed chairs, microfilm readers, a few ancient-looking desktop computers and a small stack of rectangular implements which Dr Boland explained were magnifying lamps.

"We had the whole of the Chancery collection brought

in, ma'am, as well as the State Paper Office records and the records for every judicial division," she said, pointing to a dozen metal trolleys filled with papers which had been crammed into one corner of the room.

Isabel noticed the harried look on the woman's face and rewarded her with a small smile. "Thank you for organising this at such short notice, Dr Boland. And thank you too, Professor Dunham, for dropping everything and coming out here so quickly. I appreciate it."

"My pleasure, ma'am." Dunham laid his briefcase on a desk and released the clasps, revealing several thick textbooks inside. "I brought a few key texts for reference," he explained. "What is it that Your Majesty would like to know, exactly?"

In the car, Isabel had mentally rehearsed a story which, even if leaked to the press, wouldn't cast the Crown in a negative light. Not that she couldn't deal with negative publicity, if it came to it, but it was a headache. Besides, having always lived in the spotlight as the eldest child of a king, Isabel had grown accustomed to protecting her own privacy as a matter of course.

"I'm writing a memoir," she lied. "My agent thought there should be a chapter about the use of the royal prerogative throughout my reign. I want to include some historical context comparing the use of the prerogative in the past and its use today. I had an engagement at Kew Gardens this morning and I realised that I should probably take the opportunity to look through the Crown archives, too. I'm sorry I didn't think of it until the last minute."

"As am I," Cecilia added, catching on. "I should have thought of it, really. I apologise."

At the mention of a royal memoir both Dr Boland and Professor Dunham had perked up, but Isabel fended off their questions by insisting that unfortunately the information was still commercially sensitive, as several big publishers were vying for the book. Both scholars swore that they would keep the secret.

"Your Majesty didn't need to come in person, though," Professor Dunham observed with a glint in his eyes, spotting the chance to grab a share of the profits. "I would be happy to provide Your Majesty with research assistance. I've done it several times before."

"Thank you, Professor," Isabel replied with the sweetest smile she could muster, "but as I said, I was in the area. Don't worry, though – you'll be compensated for your work today. I'm not expecting you to work for free."

Dunham blushed and started to protest that of course he hadn't been thinking about money, but the Queen waved his protestations aside. "Could you talk me through some of the less frequently used royal prerogatives?" she asked. "I want to figure out if there are any I haven't used before. I'm sure there must be. That would make my agent happy."

"Well, let's see ..." Dunham extracted a thick volume from his briefcase and leafed through it for a few moments. "There's the power to disband the army – I'm not sure if that one's ever been used, ma'am. It doesn't strike me as very useful, unless a monarch particularly wanted to incite a foreign invasion."

"Right." Isabel made a show of glancing at Cecilia to check that she was making notes, but inwardly she knew that they needed to keep going. Disbanding the army would only create problems, not solve them. "What else?"

"The royal prerogative of mercy, ma'am?"

"I used that one about ten years ago, Professor. To pardon Angela Jones, who performed CPR on her cellmate and saved her life."

"Yes, of course, ma'am." The blush on Dunham's cheeks intensified, and Isabel started to wonder whether he really was the best that UCL could offer. Perhaps she should have delayed her little outing by a few days and given Cecilia time to find a more expert … expert. Or was Professor Dunham simply one of those people who lost all their wit and went weak at the knees in the presence of their Queen? She seemed to have that effect on a lot of people, after all.

"Ah, here we go," Dunham announced, having spent perhaps a minute leafing through his textbook with a deep frown on his forehead. "How about prorogation, ma'am?"

"The prorogation of Parliament, you mean?"

"Yes, ma'am. I don't know if it's exactly what Your Majesty was looking for, because it's a prerogative that's actually exercised every year, but these days it's done by a delegation of Privy Counsellors, of course. It was last done in person by Queen Victoria in …" Dunham ran his finger along the page until he found his place again. "1854, ma'am. It could be a little anecdote in Your Majesty's memoir, with the description of how the ceremony goes today – the Peers doffing their hats, the Commons bowing and Black Rod banging on the door. People love that kind of thing, ma'am."

Isabel was already regretting thinking poorly of Professor Dunham. This could work! "Could you tell me a bit more about this prerogative, please?" she asked. "Why did Queen

Victoria stop exercising it in person?"

"Apparently she disliked the ceremony, Your Majesty."

This seemed so petty that Isabel nearly burst out laughing. "Really? But if that's the reason, surely another monarch could just start exercising this prerogative directly again?"

"Well, ma'am, the convention is that once a royal prerogative is delegated to the government it is not exercised personally by the sovereign again. Royal prerogatives are residual, ma'am."

"But doesn't the government exercise this prerogative on behalf of the Crown?" Cecilia intervened. "If there's been no Act of Parliament taking that power away from the Crown, surely Her Majesty could take it back for Herself. Hypothetically, of course," she added after Isabel shot her a warning glance.

Professor Dunham immediately launched into a detailed exploration of the legal difference between the Queen, the Crown and the Queen-in-Parliament, extracting more textbooks from his briefcase and quoting from them to illustrate his argument. These three concepts had, unsurprisingly, been the subject of much legal speculation, and although some conclusions seemed to have been reached, on the whole Isabel got the impression that their nature was still literally up for debate.

The Queen was reminded of Cecilia's words when they had been discussing the possibility of Harold Stone becoming Prime Minister: *Your Majesty forgets that we don't have a constitution.* Dunham had said it himself, not ten minutes before: the *convention* was that a royal prerogative, once delegated, would not be exercised by the sovereign in person again. There was no written law preventing it – and anyway, Isabel mused, the Crown could do no wrong. Her knowledge of the so-called constitution might have been patchier than could be expected up until now, but she definitely remembered that much.

While Professor Dunham talked, Dr Boland had started browsing the trolleys of materials, and she returned with several documents containing a host of information about the last direct use of the royal prerogative, including a juicy line from Queen Victoria's journal describing the Ex-Rajah of Coorj, who had been in the public gallery at the House of Lords during her speech, as "good for nothing".

Isabel professed her gratitude, checked with Cecilia that she had taken down all of Dunham's arguments and references and then made her excuses, assuring both scholars that her literary agent would be very pleased and offering Professor Dunham a lift back to Central London in the Bentley for his trouble, which he readily accepted. It was therefore not until they were back inside Buckingham Palace that Isabel and Cecilia were free to look at each other and burst out laughing with uncharacteristic familiarity and lack of restraint.

"Good job, ma'am," Cecilia said with a grin once she had managed to regain her composure. "I think Your Majesty might have missed Her vocation as an actor."

"On the contrary," Isabel replied. "I feel like I'm acting every day."

* * *

While the Queen and her entourage were busy with their research, on the other side of London Alice was fussing around the Hackney student house she shared with Emery and a couple of others, scrubbing floors and surfaces clean, rearranging the cushions on the sagging corduroy sofa and making sure that the mugs with fewer chips and tea stains were at the front of the cupboard.

As she checked for the third time that the fairy lights in her bedroom did not need new batteries, Alice caught herself and smiled self-mockingly. Why was she going to so much trouble? Matilda was coming over to look at textbooks, and that was that. She had given no indication that she found Alice attractive, either in person at the demo or later when they'd texted to arrange her coming over for the books. For all Alice knew, Matilda might not be into women at all. Cora had been no help in finding out one way or the other – apparently, Matilda had not been seen hanging around UCL with partners of any gender.

Alice thought about the wide-eyed young woman from the demo and realised that this wasn't surprising. Matilda had seemed very shy, almost withdrawn, and it was definitely unusual for her not to be on any social media. Even Alice's grandparents had WhatsApp and Facebook. Alice didn't mind this – she herself mostly used social media for her activism and hadn't posted anything personal in weeks apart from announcing her new job – but it made Matilda seem remote, almost otherworldly. It was surprising that the young woman had joined SRD and come along to the demo, though Alice was certainly very glad that she had.

Deciding that she had done all the housework she could, Alice set about applying some eyeliner and mascara to make her dark-brown eyes and long lashes look extra intense. She didn't normally bother with make-up, but today she felt like changing things up a little.

Finally, she rubbed some shea butter into her scalp and grabbed her favourite detangling comb. She had just started dragging the comb through her deep-brown coils when the doorbell rang. Tossing the comb aside and giving her Afro a quick pat-down instead, Alice ran to open the door.

Matilda was wearing a flowing yellow summer dress which hugged the curve of her breasts, a pair of strappy tan leather sandals and a large bright-green leather satchel. Her cheeks were slightly flushed from the mid-May sunshine, and she looked even lovelier than the first time they'd met.

"Hi! Come in," Alice said, standing aside to let Matilda through. Her heartbeat sped up as the other woman walked past her, and Alice had to remind herself that this wasn't a date. *She's just here to hopefully buy some books off you. Get a grip, Alice.*

"I like your bag," Alice added – that seemed like neutral enough territory.

"Thanks. My mum bought it for me when we went shopping in Covent Garden." Matilda glanced at Alice's bare feet and took off her sandals, placing them neatly side by side near the door. "I thought it might be a good bag for books," she added.

"Right. Books. This way." Alice led Matilda into the living room while silently berating herself. *Have you forgotten how to speak in complete sentences, Alice?* one half of her brain snarled. *But why does she have to be so cute?* complained the other half.

"There you go." Alice pointed to the coffee table in

front of the sofa, where she had laid out her old textbooks. "Tea?" she asked as Matilda took a seat. "My housemate bought this chocolate and chilli tea, if you want to try some. It's really good."

"Sure, thanks. I like spicy stuff. I mean ..." Matilda blushed and gave a nervous laugh.

"I get it. So do I." Alice smiled and then took herself off to the kitchen at speed. *Why did she blush? Is she into me too? Am I imagining things?*

Alice was grateful for the slow, cheap kettle which bought her a few minutes to herself. She took a deep breath and resolved to be careful not to make Matilda uncomfortable. The young woman was only in her first year of uni, which meant that she could easily be as young as nineteen. That was only two years younger than Alice herself, but uni changed you. Alice was a young professional now, about to step into her first full-time job after the summer. Matilda may well be one of those late bloomers who didn't really come into themselves until sometime in their twenties.

When Alice got back to the living room, she saw that Matilda had piled a few books onto one corner of the table and was now examining another thick volume. "I'll take these," she said, pointing to the pile. "Next year is mostly going to be about property law and tort. Oh, the joy," she added, rolling her eyes.

Alice laughed. "Here, tea will help you cope," she joked, placing a mug and a bottle of milk on the table. "Seriously, though, I recommend plenty of tea. And coffee. It's the only way you'll get through tort law."

"I bet. I wish I had an excuse to buy this off you." Matilda pointed to the thick book she had been looking at. "It seems way more interesting, but I don't get to do environmental law until third year. Anyway, don't you want to keep it for your new job?"

Alice sat down next to Matilda and looked at the book: *Environmental Law and Justice in Context.* The cover featured an almost abstract illustration which reminded Alice of something Picasso might have painted – not that she knew all that much about Art History. It was a more beautiful cover than those on most Law textbooks, anyway.

"Yes, you're probably right. I hadn't thought about it, but I guess textbooks are for work, too, not just uni." Alice looked through the remaining textbooks and set aside another two which also concerned environmental law.

"You're so lucky," Matilda said with a sigh. "You get to go off and fight the bad guys, and meanwhile I'm going to be stuck in a lecture theatre learning about contracts and freeholds. I wish I could come with you."

"Really? You want to work in environmental justice too?"

"I think so." Matilda had been leafing through the textbook as they talked, and now landed on a chapter about international laws surrounding access to water. "Like, I was watching a documentary by David Attenborough the other day, and apparently the supply of fresh water around the planet is becoming more unpredictable for a whole load of animals, humans included. And a lot of it is our own fault, of course. It's just so unfair, isn't it?" Matilda's light-brown eyes were shiny.

"Yes, it is," Alice said softly. Hoping that this wouldn't freak her new friend out, she shuffled closer to Matilda and put an arm around her shoulders.

Matilda stiffened for a moment, but then relaxed again and snuggled into Alice's side, resting her head on Alice's chest. "I'm sorry," she said in a small voice. "You must think that I'm a big baby."

"No, I don't. I'm the same as you." Alice stroked Matilda's shoulder and arm. "People call us 'social justice warriors' and think that we're always angry, but a lot of the time I'm just heartbroken. I mean, I'm angry about a lot of things, too, but it's more than anger, for me – I get so sad at how people treat each other and the planet."

"Me too!" Matilda turned her head so they were staring into each other's eyes. "Sometimes I just want to cry about everything."

Up close, Alice could see that Matilda had long, thick eyelashes framing her big brown eyes. One lash had fallen and come to rest at the top of Matilda's pink cheek, and Alice reached out with her index finger and picked it up. "Did you use to play that game too?" she asked.

"No." Matilda had flinched in surprise at Alice's gesture, but she hadn't seemed bothered by it. "What game?"

"The eyelash game. A friend of mine taught it to me when I was in primary school. You pick up a lash and put it on the tip of your finger, and the other person presses their finger onto yours. Whoever ends up with the lash makes a wish and then blows the lash away, and that makes the wish come true." Alice held her finger out.

"That's cute," said Matilda, pressing her fingertip against Alice's. They stayed like that for perhaps three seconds, and Alice felt a jolt travel through her. When Matilda lifted her finger, the lash stuck to it.

"There you go. I was hoping it would be you,"

Alice murmured.

Matilda gave her a small smile, then closed her eyes for a moment and blew the lash away. When she opened her eyes again but did not move away, Alice decided to try her luck. She leaned forward, and their lips met in a soft, drawn-out kiss.

So, she is *into me, after all!* Alice pulled back to take a breath and glanced at Matilda, who was smiling more broadly now, her cheeks red.

"I was hoping you would do that," Matilda said softly. Alice took that as an invitation to kiss her again.

* * *

Isabel had just finished eating dinner and was about to settle down to watch a spy drama film – her favourite kind – when her equerry knocked lightly on the door and entered the room.

"Don't tell me," Isabel snarled even before Major Phillips had straightened up from his bow. "The Ravenmaster is here again and needs to see me urgently."

"Well – yes, Your Majesty," Major Phillips said tentatively, as if worried that the Queen's fury was about to be unleashed upon him. So many people did that around her – always tiptoeing and speaking in murmurs, backing out of the room as soon as possible and never quite looking her in the eye. What did they think was going to happen? Maybe that Isabel would turn medieval on them and have their heads chopped off, like a real-life version of the Queen of Hearts from *Through the Looking Glass*?

"Let him in," Isabel grumbled. She might as well get this over and done with – then she would be able to enjoy her film in peace.

Maloney stooped lower than ever before. "Your Majesty, I'm sorry," he murmured. "I—"

Isabel cut him off. "Which one?" she asked curtly. There were only two ravens left by now, and the Queen remembered their names from her visit to the Tower the previous day. Never in her life had Isabel, who hadn't been particularly interested in house pets even as a child, thought that she would come to know a pair of ravens by name. Life really did throw some strange curveballs from time to time.

"Cressida, Your Majesty." The Ravenmaster stood stiff, his upper body tense and bent, and Isabel saw his eyes well up for a moment. Maloney wiped a tear discreetly before it could make its way down his corvid-like nose.

"Are you quite alright, Mr Maloney?" The Queen mentally crossed her fingers that the Ravenmaster wasn't about to break down into sobs in the middle of her sitting room. Her film was waiting, and it had been a very long day. A very long week, really, and they were only four days into it.

"Y-Yes, ma'am," Maloney stuttered. "I'm sorry, ma'am. It's just ... there's only Ron left now. He's the last one. The last raven of the Tower of London."

"Of course. And what of the Tower itself?" Isabel ventured to ask. "Any news there?"

The Ravenmaster flinched and gulped visibly. "The northwestern turret has collapsed, ma'am. Mr Steele has no idea how it could have happened. He said the damage didn't look anywhere close to severe enough for a collapse yesterday. And now two more large cracks have appeared, ma'am - one in each of the two remaining turrets."

"I see."

An uncomfortable silence descended upon them, extending in the space between where the Queen was sitting – slightly reclined on an antique, original Chippendale sofa, its cotton cream-coloured cushions intricately embroidered with floral silk patterns – and where the Ravenmaster was standing with his hands nervously clasped behind his curved back, his eyes fixed on the tip of a stylised flower in the middle of the burgundy Bokhara rug, his booted feet wearing a nervous pattern into the thick combed wool without his knowledge. Two people, enveloped by the same lusciously furnished room, irrevocably divided by chance of birth, and yet joined again in the knowledge that something strange and momentous was unfolding before their eyes, and that they were both – Queen and subject, servant and mistress – powerless to stop it.

"Well ..." Isabel started to speak, then realised that she had no idea what she wanted to say. She supposed she should feel angry at Maloney, at Colonel Burgess, at Anthony Steele for their incompetence. But it was clear to her, at the same time, that these events – both the ravens' flights and the cracks and collapses in the White Tower – were out of human hands and into the hands of – what? Fate?

What Isabel felt, instead of anger, was nothing but an inner emptiness which she recognised as resignation. It wasn't a feeling that she was particularly used to, having always had both an incredibly resolute and stubborn disposition and the means to make the vast majority of her whims come true. But certain things are out of the hands even of queens.

"Go home, Ravenmaster," Isabel said eventually. She acknowledged Maloney's parting bow with a nod of her head, rang for her usual cup of chamomile tea and decided that she might as well settle down to watch her spy film as planned.

* * *

Harold arrived home just as Mavis was taking a casserole dish out of the oven. "Fish pie with peas," she announced, pouring two glasses of white wine. "I fancied something a bit substantial – I went out for lunch with Tilly today to a new salad bar in Soho, and the food there was all very healthy, but not exactly filling."

"How is Tilly?" Harold asked as he hung up his coat. His brother's daughter had moved to London for university, and Harold and Mavis had promised Craig that they would keep an eye on her.

"I thought she looked a bit shifty, actually," Mavis replied. "When I asked her what she'd been up to recently she kept saying 'nothing much'. Do you think she's lonely?"

"I don't know. Maybe she's got herself a lover and doesn't want her aunt to know!"

"Harold!" Mavis swatted him playfully with a tea towel. "Anyway, you're probably right. Let's eat." Mavis served two generous portions and carried the plates to the kitchen table.

"This looks wonderful. Thank you." Harold gave his wife a kiss and a grateful hug. "Someday soon I'll be the one to cook again. And to take this one out for her walks," he added, scratching behind their dog Lana's ears.

"Don't worry, love. I knew this was going to happen back when you first stood for MP. It's a good job I enjoy it, because I bet you'll never get the chance to cook while you're Prime Minister."

Harold sank into his usual chair and took a long sip of wine before replying, "Well, that might not be for very long. I tried to resign today."

"What?" Mavis nearly dropped the pepper grinder she was carrying. "What do you mean, you *tried* to resign?"

"The Queen wouldn't accept my resignation. She told me to sleep on it and that I'd feel different in the morning Also something about having a government in place to face up to Russia." Harold ate a forkful of fish pie. "Mmmh, this is excellent."

Mavis, on the other hand, seemed to have completely forgotten the food in front of her. "Harold, why did you do that?" she asked in a strangled voice. "You've been in power less than a week! What got into you?"

"It's complicated." Harold decided that if he was going to have yet another conversation about Prince Alexander's fake letter, he would drain half his glass of wine first. "I'm going to lose the confidence of Parliament, Mavis. They wanted me to handle the threat from Venezuela, but there is no threat."

Over the next ten minutes, in-between forkfuls of food and sips of wine, Harold explained the previous day's revelations to his wife, who had already been asleep when Harold had staggered home. Mavis was so shocked that he had to remind her to eat several times.

When he got to the part of the story about his failed resignation, Harold felt goosebumps appear on his arms.

"The Queen asked me if I was a decisive leader, Mavis," he said. "I nearly panicked. All this time, and I nearly panicked."

Mavis gently placed a hand on Harold's arm. "And what did you say?"

"I told her I was. What else was I supposed to do? I feel like such a fraud," Harold admitted. "I'm not a decisive leader. I'm no kind of leader. I knew I shouldn't have let Rob talk me into becoming president of the party. It was a stupid idea." Harold felt himself blush and took another sip of his wine to calm himself down.

"Harold, look at me." Mavis kept her hand on Harold's arm, but her voice took on a sharper edge. "You *are* a leader," she said once Harold was looking into her eyes. "Did you not fly all the way to Cornwall yesterday to give the Prince of Wales a piece of your mind?"

"Yes, that's true," Harold admitted. "That felt so good, Mavis. I felt ... I don't know, brave, I suppose. Bold. Not like I am with the Queen."

"Yes, well, I haven't met Prince Alexander, but he doesn't sound like the most authoritative figure around. He sounds like an overgrown schoolboy." Mavis laughed, and Harold let himself be drawn along too.

"He is. Even his mother talks about him that way. But as soon as I was back at Buckingham Palace, I felt like *I* was the naughty schoolboy. I can't be a strong leader if I feel like that, can I?"

"Well, she's the Queen," Mavis observed. "I think a lot of people would feel intimidated by her. I probably would too."

"It's not just that, though, Mavis." Harold picked up his wine glass again and noticed that his hands were shaking slightly, as they always did when he was nervous.

"I know that I can't be trusted to be a good leader, and so do you. It's one thing being the co-director of a small company, or the president of a tiny political party that nobody's ever heard of. But Prime Minister? I don't know what I was thinking when I accepted the job." Harold sank further into his chair and drained his glass, closing his eyes and starting to rub his temples in an attempt to ease his exhaustion.

"Look at me, Harold," Mavis said again. She was using the same determined tone she always used when trying to convince him of something, and Harold knew that she wouldn't let up until she'd had her say. Reluctantly, he opened his eyes and looked at his wife.

"You are a military man, Harold Stone," Mavis continued. "Let me finish," she added when Harold tried to protest. "You went to military school *and* to Dartmouth. You have experience of combat. One mistake doesn't make you less of a leader."

At Mavis's words, Able Rate Geoffrey McNeal knocked at Harold's consciousness again. Suddenly Harold could smell the smoke again, hear the blaring sirens sounding the alarm, too little, too late.

"It wasn't just any little mistake, Mavis," he whispered. "A man died. One of *my* men." Saying the words out loud sent a shiver through Harold's body.

"I know, Harold." Mavis had lowered her voice as if out of respect for the memory of McNeal, but her tone betrayed a stab of impatience. "Do you know how many men your father lost when he was in the war?" she continued tartly. "He didn't let that stop him from doing his duty, did he? Perhaps you should try to be a bit more like him."

A weight settled on Harold's chest, making his breath laboured, and he glanced at his wife in disbelief. "Thanks very much, Mavis," he spat. "Good to know you're still on my side."

"Harold, there are no sides!" Mavis huffed in reply. "I'm just saying, your father set a great example, and you haven't exactly followed it."

The weight on Harold's chest became heavier. "If you wanted a great military man for a husband, maybe you should have married my brother," he snarled.

"Oh, for goodness' sake, Harold." Mavis stood up sharply and started gathering the dirty dishes, letting them clang against each other as she piled them up. "I'm not having this conversation with you if you're going to behave like that," she announced, carrying the dishes to the sink and starting to stuff them into the dishwasher at speed.

Harold let her get on with clearing the table and took himself off to his favourite armchair in the living room, recognising that Mavis wanted a few minutes away from him, and was using the loading of the dishwasher as a convenient excuse.

As he sat on the well worn yellow wingback chair, which had already been 'vintage' when they'd bought it from Portobello Market three decades earlier, Harold played with a loose thread on the arm and thought about what Mavis had said. It was certainly true that his late father, Commodore Aldwyn Stone, had been a war hero; no family gathering had passed without him repeating three or four of his stories about his men narrowly avoiding capture or some other disaster because of his skilful leadership. The Commodore had insisted on both his sons attending the Duke of York Military School and then naval officer training at Dartmouth, with only a brief reprieve in-between the two for the pursuit of a bachelor's degree.

Harold, the eldest, had found himself a sub lieutenant and a marine engineer officer at the age of twenty-three, put in charge of a team of fellow engineers on the HMS Loxley thanks to his Engineering degree from Bristol. Frazzled from the plunge back into military life after three relatively peaceful years at university, he had been glad of a quiet first year as an officer, keeping the ship's engine room ticking along and getting to know the rest of the crew. Then, out of the blue, the Falklands War had started.

Harold's younger brother Craig, who had been in his final year of a Physics degree at York, had been chomping at the bit to play his part in the conflict, and would have enlisted in the Navy had their mother not put her foot down and insisted that Craig sit his exams and finish his course. Harold, on the other hand, had resented his ship's summons to the front and the interruption of his comparatively quiet life.

When an Exocet missile had struck the HMS Loxley, causing a fire in the engine room, it had taken Harold and his team an abnormally long time to realise what had happened due to a fault in the communication line. As it turned out, Harold's laissez-faire attitude towards keeping the watertight doors closed had allowed the fire to spread much further than it should have done. Almost everyone had managed to evacuate the smoke-filled engine room, but one of the engineers, Able Rate Geoffrey McNeal, had been the furthest from the emergency exit and had died of suffocation.

Edward Smith, a midshipman, had unwillingly taken the fall when the lieutenant investigating the incident had incorrectly deduced that Smith had been the last person to pass through the door in question and fail to close it. Harold, riddled with guilt towards both Smith and McNeal, had returned to the UK in a deep depression and had been discharged on medical grounds, which had made him a pariah in the eyes of both his veteran father and his eager brother.

They hadn't been impressed with Harold's decision, once his condition had finally improved a little, to enrol in a Master's degree in Aeronautical Engineering at Imperial College ("You've already got one degree, what do you need another one for?" his father had barked); to found a company specialising in missile technology and ballistics out of a desire to prevent what had happened on the Loxley repeating itself ever again ("Are you playing at being an officer because you got too scared to do the real thing?" Craig had laughed); to join the Enterprise Party and eventually stand for president, officially to encourage entrepreneurship in younger people, unofficially because he was bored ("What's wrong with the Tories?" had been Harold's father's reaction); or even to become an MP ("Mostly Pen-pushing", his brother had called it). Commodore Stone had been buried to an eleven-gun salute over a decade ago, but Craig – by now a Captain – had even laughed when Harold had called him to announce that he was now Prime Minister; through the phone, Harold had heard him whisper "he won't last a week" to his wife.

Just thinking about all this made a wave of dejection

sweep through Harold's body, leaving him floppy and hunched in his chair. And yet ... hadn't the majority of the party chosen him as their president? Hadn't his constituents trusted him to represent their best interests, despite his party's minuscule size and Harold's rather late entry into politics? Hadn't the Queen – *the Queen!* – chosen him to head the government when the main parties had come to a standstill?

Feeling an unexpected surge of confidence course through him, Harold got up from his armchair and went to find Mavis. "You're right," he told her, grabbing a tea towel from her hands and starting to dry their wine glasses. "I mean, it hurt when you told me that I should be more like my father, but you're right. I have been chosen as a leader multiple times, and if the Queen herself believes that I am what this country needs, then perhaps she's right. What do you think?"

Mavis threw her arms around her husband and gave him a kiss and a tight squeeze. "Of course she is, my love. You are exactly what this country needs."

FRIDAY

"We now come to the motion of no confidence in Her Majesty's government, the motion in the name of the Leader of the Opp ... Well ..."

A chorus of laughter rose from all sides of the Commons Chamber.

"Order!" the Speaker called. "The motion in the name of the Honourable Member for Walthamstow," she corrected herself. "The Honourable Member to move the motion. Ms Caroline Banerjee."

Ms Banerjee rose swiftly and spoke with barely disguised contempt. "Thank you, Madam Speaker. I move the motion that this House has no confidence in Her Majesty's government."

The words cut straight to the pit of Harold's stomach, making it clench. Next to him on the front bench, Harold felt Rob stiffen and tighten his fist, though they both kept their backs straight and their gaze neutrally ahead.

Harold had been steeling himself for this moment for the past two days and had already had to sit through Ms Banerjee's announcement that she had tabled this motion the previous day, an announcement which had been greeted by cheers and 'Hear, hear!'s throughout the House. The now customary Cabinet members' gathering in the Sport and Social had taken on a glum and maudlin tone the previous afternoon, and even having four glasses of wine with Mavis during and after dinner – a rarity for them both – hadn't helped. Now, a hangover headache added to Harold's dejected mood and made it difficult for his befuddled brain to follow Ms Banerjee's speech.

Harold did not know whether to feel insulted or relieved that the speech was brief and mostly unchallenged. Fragments of it broke through his headache: "the Prime Minister has been party to a fabrication ..." "shameful deception of our constituents ..." "should have had the decency to resign". At one point, Rob stood to make a point, but Ms Banerjee barely spared him a glance, declared: "I will not give way," and carried on. As Rob resumed his seat Harold gave him a small pat on the back in gratitude.

It was the Queen's voice, rather than Ms Banerjee's, which resonated most clearly in Harold's mind. *You have impressed me ... I think you might be exactly what this country needs. A decisive leader ...* It had been easy to believe her in the comfort of his own home, bolstered by Mavis's tough love and faith in him; it was harder to maintain that confidence when surrounded by 648 hostile MPs. Yes, the Queen had said that the situation could be dealt with, but how?

I'm sorry, Your Majesty, Harold told her again in his imagination. *I'm not the leader You think I am. I have failed – again ...*

"The question is that this House has no confidence in Her Majesty's government. The Prime Minister."

It took a few seconds and a nudge from Rob for the Speaker's words to register in Harold's brain. He rose wearily, feeling the full weight of sixty-three years spent sitting too much and exercising too little. "Madam Speaker," he croaked, glancing at the counter-speech that he had written himself and already forgotten, "this government has barely even been given a chance to do its job—"

"That's because it's *not* doing its job!" the Conservative Member for Ipswich shouted from the back.

"Order!" Dame Margaret called again, though Harold could tell that her heart wasn't really in it. He didn't blame her: as much as the Speaker of the House was supposed to be above party allegiances, Harold suspected that he would have been equally unimpressed with her, had their roles been reversed.

"We have been in government less than a week," he continued, "and we acted according to the public interest. As soon as I became aware that there wasn't in fact a military threat from Venezuela, I informed Her Majesty—"

"He informed his mate down the pub!" Ms Banerjee yelled, standing up again.

"Order!" Dame Margaret called with more vigour. "The Honourable Member for Walthamstow knows the procedures of this House."

Ms Banerjee reluctantly sat down again, while Harold took advantage of the interruption to take a long swig of water and wipe the moisture from his forehead. Making speeches with a hangover was no joke.

"I informed Her Majesty the Queen," he repeated. "And the first thing the Foreign Secretary and I did yesterday morning was write to the Venezuelan government and their embassy in this country to express our deepest apologies for the misunderstanding." Harold took another sip of water.

"What our country needs now is time to regroup. To think of the future and what we want from it, and then make that happen. We've had five years of lackadaisical policymaking." Harold found Alan Fivecoat's tired face in the crowd and shot him a 'sorry-old-boy-just-trying-to-save-my-hide-here' look, which the former Prime Minister acknowledged with the tiniest of nods. "It's time to make bold decisions, and my government's fresh outlook is exactly what's needed."

Harold sat back down with a sigh and ran a hand over his forehead and through what remained of his hair. Ms Banerjee immediately stood up again and launched into a rebuttal speech which Harold barely bothered to pay attention to. He knew his party had no chance; his own speech had been tired and trite, and with everything else going on he and Rob hadn't had much chance to forge alliances with their fellow MPs. They didn't have a patch on Caroline Banerjee, who had been Leader of the Opposition for five years and an MP for twenty, and was a gifted speaker and a skilled organiser. Harold might not agree with many of her policy suggestions, but he had to admire the woman's talent.

Ms Banerjee spoke for several minutes, arguing – at least in the snippets that reached Harold's muddled consciousness – that to keep the Enterprise Party in government would amount to a complete and utter disregard for democracy. Rob valiantly challenged her again, but although he presented a valid enough counter-argument – that it was democracy as expressed through the laws and customs of the country that Parliament owed allegiance to, and none of them had been broken – he was drowned out by opponents on all sides.

Soon, Dame Margaret called the House to order again in preparation for voting. *This is it*, thought Harold. *Goodbye, Downing Street. It's been a pleasure – kind of.*

"The question is," the Speaker announced, "that this

House has no confidence in Her Majesty's government. As many as are of that opinion say—"

"Stop!"

650 startled faces, Harold's included, turned towards the entrance to the Chamber. There stood a diminutive woman, with long black curls which looked sightly dishevelled. Harold was too far to see her face clearly, but although she was not wearing her ceremonial uniform, he recognised her from the distinctive metal pole in her hand. She was Dame Masouda Billet, Lady Usher of the Black Rod.

"Madam Speaker," Dame Masouda said, panting slightly, "the Lord Speaker sent me with an urgent message which just reached us from Buckingham Palace." She paused to take a deep breath. "Parliament has been prorogued."

The Chamber stilled into a second of stunned silence, then everybody started talking at once. Dame Margaret's face contorted into a frown, deep lines appearing on her forehead, two bones jutting out from her tense, thin neck.

"Order!" she called loudly after a few moments. "Dame Masouda, I'm afraid I don't understand. What do you mean, Parliament has been prorogued? It's the middle of May. We were about to vote on a confidence motion."

Dame Masouda pursed her lips and nodded. "I know. That's what we all said, too. But the message is genuine, Madam Speaker. It was delivered personally to the Lord Speaker by Her Majesty's private secretary, and it has been confirmed by the Queen Herself. I heard it from the Queen myself, just before I was sent here."

Talk bubbled up again, and Dame Margaret had to

shout to quell it. "What do you mean, you heard it yourself?" she asked once the Chamber was more or less quiet again. "Were you summoned to Buckingham Palace?"

"No, Madam Speaker. The Queen is here in Parliament. She's in the House of Lords."

A collective gasp rose from the bewildered MPs, who again started talking all at once. This time, no amount of shouting and admonishing from the Speaker could silence them.

The hubbub continued for two or three minutes, with Dame Margaret sitting up in her chair at one end of the chamber, looking baffled, and Dame Masouda standing at the other end, the look on her face flicking constantly between sympathy and impatience.

Finally, Caroline Banerjee's voice rose above the general noise: "Madam Speaker! The Fixed-term Parliaments Act 2011 forbids this! It abolished the prerogative power—"

"ORDER!" Dame Margaret yelled, having noticed that Dame Masouda's lips were moving again. "Let Dame Masouda speak!"

"Thank you, Madam Speaker. We have already looked into this. The Fixed-term Parliaments Act abolished the sovereign's prerogative power to *dissolve* Parliament. It didn't affect the prerogative power to *prorogue* Parliament. Most constitutional scholars agree on this point."

Harold saw the confusion deepen on Dame Margaret's face. "Let me speak to the Lord Speaker. I am suspending this sitting," she announced, rising from her seat. She walked the long central aisle at speed, joined Black Rod and disappeared into the Members' Lobby.

"What on Earth ...?" Rob said to Harold. "Did the

Queen just save our skin? Is she really in the Lords right now?"

"I have no idea." Adrenaline and fatigue were coming to a head in Harold's system. "I guess we're going to find out soon."

They did. Not ten minutes after her hasty departure, Dame Margaret appeared back in the Chamber, followed by Dame Masouda. While Black Rod remained by the door, the Speaker walked back up the aisle, more slowly this time, and resumed her seat.

"I have to acquaint the House that I have just spoken to Her Majesty the Queen, who is indeed in the Chamber of the House of Lords at the present time." Dame Margaret's voice was dragging, and her head was slightly hung. "Her Majesty has indeed prorogued Parliament. Carry on, Lady Usher."

Dwight Treadway, the Clerk of the House, stood up before Dame Masouda had had a chance to begin her speech. "Should I slam the doors, Madam Speaker?" he asked. "It is tradition, after all."

"I wouldn't bother, Mr Treadway," Dame Margaret replied with a shake of her head. "I think we're past that point."

The Clerk sat back down among the murmurs and headshakes of most MPs, and Black Rod made her way further into the Chamber. When she spoke, she sounded dejected but resigned.

"Madam Speaker, the Queen commands this honourable House to attend Her Majesty immediately in the House of Peers."

Dame Margaret rose without a word and made her way down from her seat again. She was joined by Black

Rod and by the Serjeant at Arms, who took the ceremonial mace from its table and led the way out of the Chamber and into the Members' Lobby, then down through the Central Lobby and into the Peers' Lobby. Various voices rose in protest and kept going throughout the processions. Harold and Rob simply looked at each other, too stunned to speak.

They followed Black Rod into the House of Lords Chamber, bowed to the Queen – who was sitting on her gilded throne at the front of the room – and went to stand behind the ornate wooden bar near the door. Harold did all this in a stupor. Behind him, all protestations stopped as his fellow MPs entered the Chamber and bowed in turn, and an eerie silence descended upon the room.

Looking at his colleagues' bewildered faces, Harold realised that they – and he himself – had been unsure of what they would find in this room. Part of them had refused to believe that the Queen was actually here, in Parliament, back so soon after opening the new session less than a week before. And yet here she was, decked once again in her fur-trimmed robe, holding her head as high as her heavy, gem-encrusted crown would allow.

"My Lords, my Ladies and Members of the House of Commons," the Queen said in a steady voice as soon as the last MPs had entered the Chamber, "the past week has been an exceptional one for the country, for Parliament, for my government and for my own family. I imagine you all know by now that last week my son, His Royal Highness Prince Alexander, received a letter which purported to be from the Venezuelan government threatening our country with military action. It has now been ascertained that the letter was a fake." Harold thought he saw Ms

Banerjee snigger behind her scarf at this point.

"It is my belief," the Queen continued, unperturbed, "that the extremely delicate diplomatic situation which this incident has caused merits the full attention of both myself and my government. Therefore, I am proroguing this Parliament to a date as yet unspecified. Once the current crisis has passed, I shall summon Parliament again. In the meantime, I thank you all for your hard work and your dedication to our country."

The Queen rose and stepped down from the dais, causing the Peers to scramble up from their benches. Harold glanced at the clock behind him: the Queen had delivered her speech inside of two minutes. It had been a Machiavellian wonder, and as the Prime Minister made his way back to the House of Commons he was filled with admiration and gratitude towards the monarch. She had rescued him in the nick of time.

* * *

Alice and Matilda were taking a break from exam revision and having lunch in a vegetarian café in Bloomsbury when both their phones started firing off WhatsApp notifications in unison. At first, they both ignored the buzzing and beeping, concentrating instead on their bowls of lentil dhal and on letting their fingers linger on each other's every time they tore off pieces of their shared naan. After receiving the fifth notification in a minute, though, Alice became fed up and took her phone out of her pocket, intending to turn it off.

"Oh, my God," she exclaimed instead, reading through the several unread messages on the Students for Real

Democracy group. “The Queen went to Parliament and suspended it. Just like that.” Alice snapped her fingers.

“What?” Matilda whipped out her own phone. “Are SRD organising another protest?”

They were. Cora, Deshad and a few other committed members had started to talk about what kind of action could be taken at short notice as soon as they’d found out about what had happened in Parliament. Alice and Matilda finished their food in a hurry and rushed to Goodge Street station, where they caught the Northern line to Embankment. By the time they reached Cromwell Green, as per their friends’ instructions, the square was lined with protesters.

“We have to stay out of the road,” Cora warned them once they had found her just in front of the statue of Oliver Cromwell. “No time to get a permit, so we’re pretending to be tourists again. Tourists who just like to shout a lot.”

“Is there even anyone in there?” Alice asked, pointing to the Houses of Parliament on the other side of the green. “Or did they all go home?”

“No idea. I haven’t exactly got a lot of experience with impromptu prorogations of Parliament, you know?” Cora retorted.

“It’s madness,” Matilda added. “Good turnout, though.”

“Yeah, and it’s not just us students, either,” Cora explained. “We’ve been getting lots of members of the public to stop as well. A lot of people are outraged – I guess it’s finally too much for them, too.”

Alice took another look around the square and saw that it was filled with people of all kinds. Many of them looked as young as your average undergraduate student, but there were also plenty of grey-haired hippies and people of all ages in-between, wearing all kinds of clothes – even several people in business suits. As Alice watched, a woman with long, straight black hair climbed on top of an upturned vegetable crate, clutching a microphone.

"Who's that?" Alice asked her friends. "She looks familiar, but I can't see her very well from here."

"Caroline Banerjee," Cora replied. "There are quite a few MPs out here, apparently, mainly Labour and Lib Dems. Deshad said that there are even some people from the Lords."

"None from the bloody Enterprise Party, I bet," Alice muttered. She saw Matilda recoil slightly and was about to ask if she was okay, but at that moment the Labour leader's voice filled the square.

"Friends! Comrades!" Caroline Banerjee shouted into her microphone. "Today is a sad day for democracy. The Queen has taken it upon herself to prorogue Parliament for the sole purpose of keeping a government with no legitimacy in power!"

Unintelligible murmurs rose from the crowd, and Ms Banerjee let them die down before continuing. "The Stone government was put in place by the monarch with one task and one task only: to eliminate a military threat from Venezuela which never existed, a threat entirely fabricated by the Queen's own son, Prince Alexander. And now the monarch has decided to interfere with democracy again, and instead of allowing the vote of no confidence in the government to go ahead she has chosen to silence us all. Citizens of the United Kingdom, we will not be silenced!"

This time the crowd's reaction was louder, with cheers

and clapping resonating through the air.

"We're not citizens, though, are we?" Matilda said to Alice and Cora. "That's the problem. We're subjects."

"Speak for yourself," Cora answered with a laugh. "I'm a Peruvian citizen, and proud!"

"Yeah, well, lucky you," Matilda grumbled. "I'm stuck with subjectdom to Her Majesty the Queen."

"*Shh!*" Alice whispered. "I want to listen."

Caroline Banerjee was talking about the action that she and other Labour MPs had hastily planned in whispers while on their way back to the House of Commons Chamber, and all through the customary re-reading of the Queen's prorogation speech by the Speaker. "This square is the site of the visitors' entrance to the House of Commons. Today, we are making it the place where the people and their elected representatives gather to challenge once again the monarch's abuse of her own power over Parliament.

"Let us not look to so-called leaders from the past, who replaced one bloodthirsty ruler with another." Ms Banerjee shot a look of contempt at Cromwell's statue. "Let us instead ask ourselves what we want the future of our country to look like. Do we want to stand by and watch as what little democratic governance we have is taken away from us? Or do we want to claim our country as truly our own?"

A cheer rose from the crowd – a louder, more committed one than Alice had heard in a long time, and she was a habitual demo-goer. "What's going on?" she said with a laugh. "Since when do people in the UK know how to protest?"

"About time," Matilda replied. "Oh, hang on," she

added, pointing to Ms Banerjee, who looked like she was going to speak again.

"Let us go to Buckingham Palace and make our voices heard!" the Labour leader concluded. "Let's show the Queen that the people of the UK will not be silenced!"

Caroline Banerjee jumped off the vegetable crate and started making her way across the square towards St James's Park, followed by her fellow MPs and then, slowly but surely, by the rest of the crowd. Alice, Cora and Matilda pushed their way through the snaking procession until they found the rest of the SRD bloc.

"Grab one each and spread yourselves out," Deshad said, passing Alice a couple of megaphones and hi-vis vests. "Banerjee's speech was rousing and all that, but we need to remind people that we don't have a protest permit, so they need to stay on the pavement and make sure they don't block the road."

"How?" Alice eyed the crowd. "There must be at least two hundred people here, and the streets of Westminster aren't exactly wide. It's going to be chaos."

"I know, but it's the only chance we've got to try and make it as far as the Palace," Deshad replied, pointing at the lines of police officers – some on horseback, some on foot and kitted out in riot gear – which had sprung up around Cromwell Green and along the side of Parliament Square towards Great George Street. "I reckon that lot are just waiting for an excuse to kettle as many of us as they can."

"Good point." Alice put on one of the hi-vis vests and handed the other one to Matilda, together with a megaphone. "Meet me at that golden statue once we get to the Palace? If we get there."

"Erm ..." Matilda had taken the megaphone and the vest, but they were hanging limply in her hand. Alice remembered how shy her girlfriend had appeared when they had first met at the last SRD demo, and reminded herself that as far as she knew this might only be the second time ever that Matilda had been at a protest.

"It's okay," Alice backtracked, taking the vest and the megaphone back and handing them to Emery, who had just caught up with the group, their sitar slung over one shoulder. "You just stick with the SRD lot, and I'll keep an eye out for you, okay? It's only a few of us who are marshalling, right, Deshad?"

Deshad nodded, and Matilda took Alice's hand and pulled her in for a long kiss.

"See you on the steps by the golden statue," Alice reminded Matilda once they had finally forced themselves to break apart. Then she waved goodbye, turned on her megaphone and made her way to the outside of the procession, sticking her tongue out at the statue of Winston Churchill as she went. While she walked, she sent Fran a quick text: *Did you hear about Parliament? Protest happening now, come over in your lunch break.*

* * *

It takes the average person fifteen to twenty minutes to walk past Parliament Square Garden, along Great George Street, then onto the pleasant Birdcage Walk by the side of St James's Park and up to the large roundabout dominated by the statue of Queen Victoria and a golden angel which sits in front of Buckingham Palace. It took the impromptu procession of MPs, students and other disgruntled subjects the best part of an hour to snake their way past the clusters of selfie-snapping tourists while leaving just enough space for the eternally busy, stop-at-nothing Londoners to march past.

Alice and her fellow marshals - mostly other students from SRD and similar organisations, joined by a few junior employees of the Labour Party's parliamentary office - spent that time running up and down the street reminding folks to remain on the pavement at all costs. Cora, Deshad and the other student politics leaders who had arrived at the Houses of Parliament first had held a hurried consultation with Caroline Banerjee and her staff, and the group had somehow accepted SRD's proposal to employ the same tactic which had proved successful in avoiding arrest at their protest against the Stone government earlier that week.

Armed with her nearly completed Law degree, Alice had spent the latter part of the SRD meeting on Tuesday morning trawling through the Public Order Act of 1986, and had come to the conclusion that a group of people who were walking on the pavement would not fit the description of either a 'procession' or an 'assembly', and might therefore get away with not having a police permit, which they would have needed to apply for two weeks prior - long before Stone's appointment. Whether this defence would hold up in court was, as with all things legal, up to debate, but as the Act did not specify a definition of 'procession' Alice had thought that they could give it a shot.

So, the students had walked to and then around the Parliament building, shouting and chanting and even drumming, but never stopping or setting foot on the road, with the mounted police officers watching them carefully but without intervening. After a couple of hours most students had got tired and preoccupied with the amount of exam revision they had to do, and the non-procession had disbanded.

Today, however, things were different. Instead of the fifty or so people that they'd managed to rustle up on Tuesday, they were now dealing with a crowd of at least two hundred, with a few curious passers-by adding to their ranks as they made their way towards Buckingham Palace. And this wasn't just a student protest, but one led by a major political figure, and which included several other MPs. By the time they made it to the front of Buckingham Palace, they were surrounded by a thick line of police officers in riot gear, with a second line of mounted officers bringing up the rear.

"Keep walking! Go around the statue!" Alice, finding herself towards the front, shouted into her megaphone, startling a cluster of tourists nearby. Spotting Cora not far behind her, she waved her friend over. "I need to find Matilda," Alice explained. "She looked a bit spooked earlier. I don't think she's been to many demos. Can you do without me for a bit?"

"Sure," Cora replied, taking Alice's megaphone and hi-vis vest.

Alice thanked her and pushed her way through the crowd to the front of the statue, scanning the various groups of people sat on the steps. She found Matilda a minute later and they shared a passionate, drawn-out kiss.

"Are you okay?" Alice asked. "Is this all a bit much for you?"

"No, no, I'm fine," Matilda replied, but she sounded worried and distant.

"Are you sure?" Alice insisted.

"Yes! I'm fine," Matilda repeated with more conviction. "So, what happens now?"

"I don't really know," Alice admitted. "I mean, other than us carrying on walking and shouting."

"It's ridiculous that we have to stay on the pavement. At least the pedestrian bit is wider here, but seriously, how are we supposed to protest something if we have to wait two weeks for a permit? By the time we get it there will be some other bullshit to protest against somewhere else."

"Yeah, it's almost as if the police didn't want people to be able to express their dissent. Oh, wait ..."

Matilda giggled, and it was such a sweet sound that Alice wanted to kiss her again. They made out for a few seconds and only broke apart when a chant erupted from the crowd, distracting them: "Down with the Queen! Up with democracy!"

"Is that Banerjee on the megaphone?" Matilda asked.

"I think so. Shall we go back over there?"

"Come on, then."

The two women turned back towards the road and saw that most of the protesters were now standing in front of the gate to Buckingham Palace. Some had even sat down on the pavement as they chanted.

"Shit!" Alice exclaimed. She ran across to the nearest cluster of sitting protesters, some of the older hippies she remembered spotting back in Cromwell Green. "Stand up!" Alice told them. "We have to keep moving!"

"Ah, chill out, love," a guy in a tie-dyed T-shirt replied. "We've been on our feet for yonks."

"I know, and I appreciate that, but not everyone here

is comfortable being kettled and arrested."

"Since when is protesting supposed to be comfortable?" a lady in an ACAB T-shirt piped up. Alice wanted to point out that they were the ones who had wanted to sit down to be more comfortable, but she figured that it would be a waste of time. Instead, she scanned the crowd for a hi-vis vest, spotting Emery and running towards them, Matilda in tow.

"What happened?" Alice breathed. "I spent a few minutes looking for Matilda and all of a sudden we've stopped."

"I know," Emery replied, rolling their eyes. "People saw Buckingham Palace and decided that we have arrived and that's it. They're not listening to us, and the Labour lot are too busy starting up chants. I mean, I know chants are important, but still."

"Shit," Alice said again. "What do we do now? Have you talked to Cora and the others?"

"No, I was about to go and find them. Shall we go together?"

"Hang on." Alice turned to Matilda. "Are you okay with staying? That lot don't look too happy," she remarked, glancing at the ranks of police officers, which had got thicker. "We might end up getting arrested."

Matilda hesitated for a couple of seconds, then took a deep breath. "It's okay, I'll stay," she declared.

Alice took her hand and squeezed it, and the three of them set off to find as many fellow SRD members as they could.

"I don't think we have much choice," said Cora once they had gathered in a huddle as far away from the chanting crowd as possible. "You know what crowds are like. They're not going to shift now unless it's to give up and go home. So, I think we either do that ourselves or stay and take our chances with the cops."

"Good luck with that," Deshad murmured.

Bella, a young woman from King's College who was standing next to Emery, spoke up in an apologetic tone. "I'm sorry, but I don't think I can stay. I really want to, but I work part-time as a babysitter and if I get charged with anything they'll take away my DBS certificate. A friend of mine wanted to start an art club for children, but her DBS was denied because she was once fined for doing graffiti. I just can't risk it."

"That's fine," Cora replied. "In fact, I think that everyone who's here and wants to stay should try and find as many people as possible from their uni and explain what the risks are again, just so people are aware. Basically, being arrested and possibly charged with some protest-related crap. Which is a fine, isn't it, Alice?"

"Yes, just a fine for people who aren't organising the protest or telling other people to join it."

"Okay. Let's do that, then, and meet up in this spot again in half an hour."

Alice and Emery were heading back towards the main group of protesters to look for other SOAS students when they were approached by a woman holding a microphone and a man with a video camera on his shoulder. "Excuse me, can I interview you for BBC News?" the woman asked.

"No, thanks," Emery murmured. As sociable and bubbly as they were with their friends, Alice knew that Emery loathed public speaking.

"It's okay," Alice told them with a laugh. "Look, I

think that's Eda over there in the hi-vis," she added, pointing towards the crowd. "Why don't you ask her to help you find the other SOAS folks? Matilda, maybe you can try and find some of the UCL people? I'll do the interview."

Emery and Matilda hurried off while the two journalists ran a sound check and adjusted the camera angle.

"I am here in front of Buckingham Palace," the woman announced into her microphone, "where a crowd has gathered to protest the Queen's unexpected prorogation of Parliament this morning. I am about to interview one of the protesters. Tell me, why exactly are you here today?"

"Because what the Queen is doing is completely undemocratic," Alice said into the microphone which had now been thrust towards her. "First she appointed a completely unknown politician as Prime Minister, and now she's prorogued Parliament only a week after the start of the new legislature. She's only doing it to save Stone's neck, and frankly we've had enough."

"And when you say 'we', who do you mean?"

"Well, I'm part of a movement called Students for Real Democracy, which is made up of people from all over the University of London, and quite a few of us are here today. But it's not just students - there are MPs protesting and a lot of other people too. Much of the opposition is on our side. Which I guess means almost everybody these days."

"And what makes you think that your tactics will be effective?"

Strangely enough, for someone who had been a key figure in student politics for the past three years and her

Students' Union campaigns officer for the past year, Alice had never been asked this question before. She took a moment to reflect, noticing the journalist shuffling her feet impatiently. Just as the interviewer was about to speak again, Alice answered. "I don't, particularly. Unfortunately, those in power have an excellent record of ignoring protesters' demands. But I don't see what other way we have of making it clear what we think about this prorogation. It's not like the Queen is holding public audiences, and I can't exactly write to my MP now, can I?"

Just as the journalist was about to ask another question, Matilda caught up with Alice, followed by a dozen of her fellow UCL students. "We're heading back over to the SRD meeting spot," she said, a nervous tremor in her voice. "Cora texted everyone. The cops look like they're getting restless. Are you coming?"

"Yes. Excuse me," Alice told the two journalists. She took Matilda's hand and squeezed it tight. "It's going to be okay," she whispered as they walked towards the SRD group. Matilda nodded, but she looked pale and unconvinced.

Once they had found their friends again, Alice checked her phone and saw a reply from Fran: *Sorry, had to take today off. Ben has chickenpox. How's it going?*

Okay for now, Alice texted back. *Might get arrested though.*

I'll come visit you in prison, Fran replied. She added a laughing emoji, but Alice did not feel much like laughing.

* * *

"Are you quite alright, Your Majesty? You look a bit tired, ma'am."

Isabel smiled at her lady-in-waiting and confidante, Lady Gillian, and took a sip of tea. "Yes, I'm fine. It's just been a long week."

Lady Gillian offered the Queen a plate of buttered scones, then took one herself. "Do you have any engagements this weekend, ma'am?" she asked as she spread a thick layer of clotted cream onto her scone, then slid the cream bowl towards Isabel and swapped it for a bowl of strawberry jam. The Queen, whose father had been the Duke of Cornwall before ascending the throne, had been mocking her friend's preference for the Devon school of scone-topping ever since their schooldays together at Wycombe Abbey. Their different methods did, however, make for pleasingly symmetrical cream teas.

"No, I don't, for once," Isabel replied, in turn busying herself with the cream. "I'm just going to go for a walk or two and catch up on some reading."

"And how are things with the new Prime Minister, ma'am?"

Isabel rolled her eyes and took a fortifying bite of her scone. "He's a bit of a wimp, honestly, Gillian. I thought he would have more of a spine than Fivecoat, but there's not much in it, really. I had to give him a pep talk yesterday to stop him from resigning."

Lady Gillian gave a small laugh. "And now you've had to go and rescue him from a no-confidence vote, ma'am. That must have been a nuisance."

Isabel considered this comment for a few moments. "Yes, it was, rather, but it was also ... I don't know. Fascinating, maybe. You know, the monarch hasn't prorogued Parliament in person since the days of Queen Victoria, so it felt good to take that tradition back. After all, I open every Parliamentary session myself, so why shouldn't I close them too?"

"Absolutely, Your Majesty." Lady Gillian refilled their teacups. "It's your prerogative, after all, ma'am. I just hope that the next Prime Minister turns out to have a little more initiative!"

"I don't know. I think I like it this way, actually. The Prime Minister listens to me and does what I tell him to, and I feel like I'm finally doing more than just signing pieces of paper and waving at crowds, you know? I'm doing what a monarch should be doing."

"Of course, ma'am. And may I ask ..." Lady Gillian trailed off, the knife she had been using to spread jam on another scone suspended in mid-air.

"What?" the Queen prompted. She and Gillian had been friends for so long that her lady-in-waiting was usually freer with Isabel than most other people. It was one of the reasons that Isabel always found their time together so refreshing.

"I was just wondering how things are with His Royal Highness Prince Alexander, ma'am," Gillian finally decided to say.

Isabel scoffed. "He did such a stupid thing. But at least I'm not as bored as I used to be, right?" The Queen laughed. "Cleaning up his mess has made me a stronger monarch than ever before, so there is that."

The two friends continued their cream tea in companionable silence, until a rumble started to filter in through the open window.

"What on Earth is that?" Isabel asked.

Gillian went to the window and peered out for a few moments, before turning back towards Isabel with a confused look on her face. "There's quite a crowd walking towards the Palace, ma'am. A lot of them are shouting, ma'am, but I can't make out what they're saying."

Isabel thought through the daily briefing she had received from Cecilia early that morning. "My assistant didn't mention any plans for a march or anything like that. Are they blocking the road?"

"No, ma'am. They're just walking on the pavement."

"Okay. Well, there's always somebody making a fuss about something or other in Central London. I'm sure they'll be gone soon."

Isabel and Gillian had no more time to devote to speculating about the nature of this unplanned gathering, for at that moment the Queen's equerry knocked on the door and quietly entered the room. "I'm sorry to disturb, Your Majesty - Lady Gillian," he said after his bow. "The Ravenmaster is here and would like an audience, ma'am."

Major Phillips had kept his tone professionally even, as usual, but Isabel noticed that his gaze wandered as he spoke, settling first on the intricate pattern on the rug, then on the empty teacups, then on the kingfisher-shaped brooch pinned on Lady Gillian's turquoise cardigan ... The equerry was doing everything he could to avoid looking at the Queen, even in passing. *He knows*, Isabel thought with a shudder. *Of course he does. Anyone can count to six. They're probably laughing behind my back, every single one of them. Either that, or they're terrified.*

With some surprise, Isabel realised that a pit had opened inside her own stomach. *Don't be silly*, she chided herself. *It's only a bit of ancient superstition. Just an old tale started by people who still believed in witchcraft and ghosts. It doesn't mean anything.*

And yet, now that the Ravenmaster had come to deliver the final blow – because that's what it had to be, surely – the Queen realised that she was feeling a measure of grief. She had managed to minimise the matter of the White Tower and the ravens until now, concentrating most of her energies on cleaning up the mess that her son had created, and then on keeping her puppet Prime Minister in place once she had realised that she enjoyed the taste of direct power. But now that all of that had been sorted, Isabel couldn't help but feel a pang of pain at the thought of being remembered as the monarch who let all the ravens fly away and the White Tower crumble to dust.

"Let him in," Isabel croaked to her equerry, her throat suddenly dry despite the copious amounts of tea she had just consumed.

Major Phillips bowed and left the room quickly, Lady Gillian rising unprompted and following suit. As she walked past the Queen to get to the door, she broke with protocol and laid a hand on her friend's arm, just for a moment.

"Thank you," Isabel murmured, shocked at her lady-in-waiting's action and even more shocked to realise how comforting it felt.

The Ravenmaster looked an even gloomier version of his usual self. It took a couple of seconds for the Queen to realise that this was due not only to the sour expression on his face, which was contorting the lineaments around his beak-like nose, but also to the fact that today Maloney was wearing a black tailcoat with matching trousers and tie in place of his bright-red Beefeater uniform. Both his hands were clutched around a cream envelope, his knuckles almost the same colour.

"What's going on, Mr Maloney?" Isabel asked, thinking back to his first appearance at the Palace the previous Sunday, when she had failed to remember his name. It seemed impossible that only five days had gone by since then; now the sight of the Ravenmaster was as familiar to the Queen as that of her equerry, or of Lady Gillian.

"Your Majesty," Maloney murmured, "I am hereby resigning from the post of Ravenmaster of Your Majesty's Royal Palace and Fortress of the Tower of London." He took a step towards the coffee table, which still held the remains of Isabel and Gillian's cream tea, and placed the envelope on it. The Queen glanced at it: an unmarked slip of paper except for a single line of neat calligraphy addressing the envelope to 'Her Majesty the Queen'.

"I see." Isabel swallowed and took a deep breath before adding, "May I ask what has caused this decision?"

Maloney's hands, now free from their burden, were clasped tightly in front of him, although this didn't entirely stop the man from fidgeting. "It's over, Your Majesty," he said, his voice cracking. "Ron was nowhere to be found this morning. The last raven has left the Tower of London."

Isabel felt the unfamiliar sensation of tears pricking her eyes and shut them for a moment. "And what of the White Tower?"

"Gone, ma'am. We all heard a huge noise around ten this morning. All three turrets and the chapel roof collapsed, and they brought the rest of the building down with them.

It's all just a pile of stones and dust now, ma'am." Maloney was now speaking so softly that Isabel had to concentrate to make out his words. He finished talking and bowed his head, his hands stilling for once, his whole body curved but rigid, as if awaiting sentencing.

Isabel thought back to her own activities earlier in the day. While the White Tower, one of the oldest and most important buildings in the country, was falling to the ground, she had been walking into the House of Lords, blissfully unaware. She hadn't heard or felt a thing. Of course, how could she? The two buildings stood at opposite ends of a huge bend in the Thames, nearly three miles apart. Yet, for some reason, Isabel found it hard to believe that such an ancient symbol of English monarchical rule had crumbled to dust without her knowledge.

"Thank you, Mr Maloney," the Queen said softly. She didn't know what else to say.

The former Ravenmaster bowed deeply before her – this time not from his neck, as was customary, but from the waist and nearly to the ground, which made Isabel feel as if she had gone back in time several centuries. She almost expected Maloney to drop down on one knee, but instead he straightened up just enough to be able to walk and inched backwards out of the room.

Outside, the crowd had not, in fact, moved on. As Isabel poured herself another cup of tea with shaky hands, a cry broke through the window: "Down with the Queen!"

Isabel didn't even have the time to stand up and go to the window to investigate before Major Phillips knocked on the door again. "Ms Drummond, Colonel Guffy and Mr Weston would like a word, Your Majesty," he announced. His voice was steady, but Isabel thought his normally florid pink complexion had paled.

"Let them in," she said quietly, resolving to ignore the headache which was now mounting an offence at her temples.

During Cecilia's three years of service, a joke had developed between them in which Isabel, whose Wycombe Abbey education had included a heavy dose of Classics, called Cecilia, Kevin Weston and Colonel Bob Guffy 'the Triumvirate'.

Guffy, the Palace's chief of security, was a bulky ex-Marine who never smiled, spoke only the minimum number of words required to communicate and conducted his business with the kind of quiet, ruthless efficiency which would have had a weaker person than the Queen quaking in their boots.

Weston, on the other hand, was a thin reed of a man, no older than thirty-five, who was constantly wiping his small rectangular glasses on his overly baggy shirts and who spoke about public relations - the field he oversaw at the Palace - with a kind of nervous passion. When he had joined the Palace's staff as the newest PR officer five years previously, Isabel had thought him far too wet behind the ears to survive long in this environment. Within six months of his appointment, however, Weston had come up with an ingenious plan to 'take control of the narrative', as he put it, after Prince Alexander had been photographed in a dubious position in an equally dubious Soho nightclub. The prince had suffered nothing more than a royal telling off from his mother, and Weston had bagged himself the promotion which had made him the youngest head of public relations the Palace had ever seen.

Whenever the Palace faced any sort of crisis, the Triumvirate came out in force. As the three of them made their bows and curtsy, Isabel rolled her shoulders back, took a deep breath and prepared herself for the onslaught of advice.

It was Cecilia who spoke first. "Your Majesty, there is a sizeable crowd of protesters outside the Palace. Mostly students and other regular people, as it were, but there are also several Members of Parliament, ma'am."

"Banerjee?" Isabel guessed.

"Yes, ma'am. Quite a few of her Labour colleagues, and a good number of Lib Dems and independents, too."

"The Lib Dems are taking a stand? I must be doing something right," Isabel deadpanned. Weston snorted in a failed attempt to suppress a laugh, and Colonel Guffy glared at him until the PR manager went quiet again and dropped his gaze.

"How many people are we talking about?" the Queen asked, turning to the chief of security.

"About two hundred, Your Majesty. The Met Police assistant commissioner informs me that there were around half that number when the crowd assembled just outside Parliament, but they must have picked up more people between there and the Palace."

"And the police didn't think to stop them before they got to my doorstep?"

Colonel Guffy looked uneasy, a first as far as Isabel was aware. "These folks are cunning, ma'am. They kept to the pavement the whole way here, and kept moving, so they couldn't be accused of organising an illegal procession or a dangerous public assembly. Apparently, the deputy assistant commissioner in charge of local policing told the units in the area to come out in force and be ready, but not to intervene unless the protesters broke the law in some way. She told the assistant commissioner that she was concerned about public opinion, ma'am."

"I see." Isabel thought for a moment before turning to the head of PR. "And what do you make of that concern, Mr Weston?"

"I share it, Your Majesty," Weston replied without hesitation. "What Your Majesty did in Parliament today is ... well ... unusual. The press is going to be all over it, ma'am, and I think it would be wise to proceed with extreme caution when it comes to the public. We don't want to endanger the image of the Crown, ma'am."

"The image of the Crown," Isabel repeated. She thought for a few moments, studying Weston's light-brown complexion. "Remind me, Mr Weston, where were your grandparents from again?"

Each December the Queen held a dinner for all heads of department at the Palace, and during the last one of these Mr Weston had told her how elated his 85-year-old maternal grandmother had been to be able to catch a glimpse of the Queen at the celebrations for the granting of a Royal Charter to her local secondary school in Wembley.

"Malaysia, ma'am," Weston replied, clearly confused by the question. "Or, well, Malaya, as they always called it. They had migrated to London by the time it became Malaysia."

"And how did the British colonial regime treat them while they were still in Malaya?"

Weston dropped his gaze again and gulped visibly. "Well ... my grandmother and her parents were put in a concentration camp, ma'am. They were told that they would be deported to India because they were Tamil. But that never happened, and a few years later my grandmother was moved to a colonial estate to work, ma'am. That's where she met my grandfather."

"I don't imagine their living conditions on the estate were luxurious," Isabel commented, silencing Cecilia and Guffy, who were clearly about to protest the abrupt change of subject, with a raised hand.

"No, Your Majesty. They lived in a shack and were always hungry and ill, from what they told me."

"So they can't have been the biggest fans of the British Empire. And yet, at the first chance they got they jumped on a plane to London, and last year your grandmother was singing *God Save the Queen* at that school in Wembley and telling all her neighbours that she'd caught a glimpse of my hat."

"Well ... yes, Your Majesty."

Isabel turned back to her chief of security. "Clear the protesters, Colonel."

* * *

"Careful! You're going to break it!"

"I've got it. Don't worry."

Harold took the green Sumida vase – a wedding present from his aunt – from Mavis's hands, unwrapped it and carefully placed it on top of the walnut sideboard which they had decided to put on the far wall of the living room, opposite the door. "There. That should be the last of it. Although I'm still amazed that you insisted on moving this vase here. I thought you liked it."

"I do like it." Mavis sat down on the divan, newly transported from their guest bedroom back in Wimbledon, and let out a small puff of air. "I like it a lot. Your aunt Roselda had excellent taste. I just thought that we should try to cheer this place up a bit. With so little space you need make a place cosy, or it will just look cramped."

"I know. You're very good at that." Harold sat down next to his wife and kissed her on the cheek.

"Well, I don't run an art gallery for nothing! Now, where did that kettle go?"

Mavis dug around for a kettle and two mugs, and Harold went downstairs and asked Tom to find them a pint of milk. When they were both sitting down again with their cups of tea and a plate of biscuits, Mavis drew another sigh and cast a look around the room. "Never in my life did I imagine I would be moving into 10 Downing Street. Well done, my love," she added, patting Harold's thigh.

"Thanks, although I can't really take the credit. You know it was all the Queen's doing." Harold took a long, pensive sip of his tea. "As was today."

"Why, what happened today?"

Harold nearly choked on his chocolate digestive. "You don't know? Haven't you seen the news? I didn't tell you because I assumed you knew."

"Harold, I took the day off to move us into here, remember? I've had no time for the news. Now, will you tell me what's happened?"

"The Queen prorogued Parliament."

This time it was Mavis who nearly choked on a biscuit. "What do you mean? The session has only just started!"

"I know. She did it to stop Caroline Banerjee and her cronies from getting a vote of no confidence through, and she did it just in time, as well. I swear, I thought my political career was over. It was a stroke of genius, Mavis. The Queen is an absolute mastermind."

"That's not what you were saying last night."

"I know!" Harold said again with a laugh. "I think I panicked. I didn't want to believe her when she told me that I am just what the country needs. Or you, when you said the same thing the night before."

"And do you believe it now?"

Harold pondered the question for several moments before replying. "Yes, I do. Look at how smoothly the whole thing went in the end. Plus, the Queen's been the Queen for a long time now. She's had a lot of Prime Ministers. If she says that I am the right person for the job, then I must be, right?"

A rush of something flooded through Harold's brain – pride? Relief? It felt like an invigorating mixture of the two. When Mavis had insisted on staking their claim on the flat at the top of 10 Downing Street as soon as the last of Alan Fivecoat's possessions had been cleared away, Harold had tried to convince her to wait, feeling that the move would be a huge waste of time, energy and money, and that they would be required to reverse it within a day or two.

Now, Harold realised that Mavis must have seen something in him, way back when they had first met as undergraduates in Bristol, where he was studying Engineering on a much needed hiatus from military education and she was reading History of Art: a kind of enduring strength of character which he didn't know himself he possessed. Otherwise, why would she had stayed with him through the failure of his military career, and endured so many sleepless nights by his side as he talked to her over and over about what had happened on the HMS Loxley and about the looks of quiet contempt which now followed him around every time he was in the presence of his father and brother? Wouldn't his wife have left him long ago for one of her artists, if she hadn't recognised more talent and resilience in Harold than he could see himself? And now the Queen must have seen the same in him. Why else would she have plucked him out of obscurity and sent him straight to the top, to sort out the mess that her country had been plunged into?

"You know," Harold said with a grin, "I think I'm ready for something stronger than tea. We should celebrate, don't you think?"

"I'll dig out a couple of glasses," Mavis replied with a glint in her eyes, disappearing through the kitchen.

Harold was about to lift the intercom receiver to ask Tom from downstairs to make a trip to the nearest off-licence, when the receptionist appeared at the door clutching his iPad, clearly out of breath from running too fast up the stairs. "Urgent message from Buckingham Palace, Prime Minister," he wheezed. "You're going to want to read this, sir."

* * *

Ten minutes later, Harold was sitting in the Queen's study, flanked by her private secretary on one side and her head of PR on the other. The Queen herself sat across from them all on the other side of her desk.

"I appreciate your concern, Prime Minister," she said shortly, having listened to Harold's hurried plea for caution, "but I don't share your preoccupation with public opinion. Mr Weston here was also at pains to persuade me that clearing the protesters will cause a problem, but frankly I don't see any evidence of that claim being true. We're not in Stuart times anymore, you know. People love the Crown."

"Until today, Your Majesty," Harold dared to point out. "There's plenty of ordinary people protesting out there, ma'am. They're clearly angry."

"The people are fickle, Prime Minister. Believe me. I've been on the throne far longer than you have been in politics. Your precious public will have forgotten all about this within the week."

"Forgive me, Your Majesty," Harold insisted, "but how can you be so sure, ma'am?"

The Queen gave a short laugh. "It's always the same few die-hards who make a fuss, Prime Minister. Listen to their arguments," she added, turning her computer screen towards Harold and tapping a few keys. "Most people don't have time for this. They've got jobs to keep and families to feed."

A video of the protest started playing, the footer identifying it as a BBC News live broadcast. A journalist was interviewing a young woman who was clearly one of the protesters. "Unfortunately," the young woman said, "those in power have an excellent record of ignoring protesters' demands. But I don't see what other way we have of making it clear what we think about this prorogation. It's not like the Queen is holding public audiences, and I can't exactly write to my MP now, can I?"

The Queen paused the video just as another protester came into the frame. "You see, Mr Stone," she said, "this woman's probably doing a degree in Politics or something like that. Most common folk won't even have a clue what 'prorogation' means, and I doubt many of them will bother to Google it. It will all die down within the next couple of days, trust me."

Harold just about registered what the Queen was saying. When she fell silent, he murmured, "Yes, Your Majesty," bowed and retreated quickly out of the room, barely even noticing the surprised stares which followed him out. The image of the second protester who had entered the camera frame on the BBC video just as the Queen had paused it – a young woman with wavy brown hair in a bob, pink cheeks and glasses – had been burnt into his mind.

As he followed the Queen's equerry down the stairs, Harold fished his phone out of his pocket and sent his brother Craig a curt text: *Come to London. Tilly's in trouble.*

* * *

"Attention!" A policeman's voice echoed through a megaphone. "This public assembly is posing a threat to public order and property. You have five minutes to disperse. If you fail to comply you will be held in breach of section 14 of the Public Order Act 1986. I repeat, you have five minutes to disperse!"

"Five minutes? What the hell do we do?" Matilda's voice had a panicked edge to it, and Alice took her hand and squeezed it while she glanced around them. They had been in front of Buckingham Palace nearly an hour now, and after making the rounds and collecting all their fellow students who had opted to remain, they had succumbed to the physical tiredness that stress brought with it and had sat down in the middle of the pedestrian road between the statue and the Palace gates, reckoning that the damage to their law-abiding plans had been done already. What Alice hadn't realised was that while she and the rest of the student bloc discussed options on how to proceed, various groups of protesters had sat down all around them, effectively blocking their path.

"I don't think we're going to make it out of here in time," Cora observed, giving voice to what Alice had been thinking, too. At least one of the allocated five minutes had already passed, with lots of murmured discussions between the protesters but only a few people at the edge of the crowd getting up and hightailing it back towards Parliament or into one of the parks.

Alice knew from her three years in student politics that this slow reaction didn't necessarily signal the crowd's commitment to defying the police orders and staying, so much as a delay in comprehending what was actually going on. Not everybody who went on demonstrations knew what to expect, and many people had yet to disabuse themselves of the notion that the British police were nothing but a bunch of friendly, harmless neighbourhood Bobbies. As a result, even just the fact of being on the receiving end of a police order, with an undefined but clear threat attached to it, took a while to sink in. *Just you wait*, Alice thought grimly.

Sure enough, four minutes into the dispersal time only about half of the people who had been sat between the SRD group and the edge of the crowd had got up and left. Alice noticed that all the MPs, many of whom had been so vocal before, were now nowhere to be seen. "Typical," she muttered to the rest of her group as she stroked Matilda's hand. "No doubt tomorrow the Labour and Lib Dem socials will be all about how they don't condone illegal protests."

"Yeah. Oh, I nearly forgot," Cora said, rooting into the pockets of her jeans and pulling out some frayed-edged cards. "I gave these out when we assembled on Cromwell Green, but that was before you got there." She gave a card each to Alice and Matilda before passing them on throughout the group, and Alice saw that it outlined basic legal advice to follow in case of arrest, as well as the phone numbers of a couple of solicitors' firms specialising in protest law.

"Does anyone have a Sharpie?" Alice asked the group. Emery dug inside their backpack and passed her a black marker pen. Alice wrote the solicitors' numbers on her arm, then gave the Sharpie to Matilda and told her to do the same.

"W-Why?" Matilda asked, her voice trembling.

Alice put an arm around her shoulders and pulled her close. "Listen, it's just a precaution in case the police take away our stuff. You have the right to speak to a solicitor if you get arrested, and the ones they have at the police station won't necessarily know the ins and outs of protest law, so it's better to call one of these. You also have the right to let someone know that you've been arrested. Do you know your parents' phone number by heart?"

Matilda's eyes widened. "I don't want my parents to know! My dad's a Navy captain. He'd never speak to me again."

Alice was pretty sure that she felt Matilda shudder. "Okay," she said, giving her girlfriend a reassuring squeeze. "Write the number for the Protest Support Line on your arm, then. I'll do the same. My parents are in Zimbabwe, so it's not like they'd be much use. Although maybe I should write down Fran's number too. I bet she'd come if I needed help."

Alice was just passing the Sharpie back to Emery when the same policeman's amplified voice broke through the tense atmosphere. "Attention! You are now in breach of section 14 of the Public Order Act 1986 and are all under arrest for failing to comply with conditions imposed by the police on a public assembly. If you try to leave now, we will have to use reasonable force to restrain you. It is in your best interest to comply."

Having busied herself with reassuring Matilda as best she could and ensuring that they both had the necessary phone numbers written on their arms, Alice hadn't been paying much attention to the changing human landscape around them. She now looked up to see that everyone who was still sitting on the ground had been surrounded by a close rank of police officers in riot gear. This was the usual technique of kettling which Alice had witnessed before, but what surprised her was seeing an outer ring of officers around the first, with maybe three yards between the two. The people making up the outer ring were not police, but Palace guards, complete with their garish red jackets and their dozen-inches-tall bearskin hats. Alice could not help but burst into laughter at that sight.

What followed was as unpleasant as it was expected. Several police vans had been parked by the statue's steps, and the two rings of guards and police officers slowly moved towards them, forcing the crowd of protesters in the middle to stand up and move with them. Anyone who was too slow to move took a truncheon to the legs, and at hearing the shrieks of those unfortunate victims Alice gave thanks that the SRD bloc had ended up in the centre. Matilda was now sobbing, and Alice concentrated on keeping them both moving while she rubbed her girlfriend's back as much as she could.

Eventually they were shoved into a van, already crammed with people. Alice recognised Cora, Emery and Deshad, as well as some of the other students who had sat near them. "You alright, babe?" Emery whispered, reaching for Alice's hand. Alice squeezed it and nodded.

Once the back doors of the van had been slammed shut, the vehicle started its slow crawl. With no windows in the back of the van, it was impossible to know which way they were going. Eventually, after what felt like an hour, but was probably more like ten or fifteen minutes, they came to a stop and the back doors of the van were opened again, causing Alice's eyes to squeezed shut as they adjusted to daylight again.

A hand pulled Alice brusquely out of the van, and she tripped and fell to the ground, hitting her knee.

"Alice!" she heard Matilda shriek.

"I'm okay," Alice called back, lifting herself up. She spotted Matilda and inched towards her in the small crowd, while a police officer barked at them to follow him in an orderly line.

"Remember, you don't have to say anything," Alice whispered in Matilda's ear as she positioned herself behind her in the line. Matilda nodded and sniffed loudly.

They were led inside the police station and sorted into two groups, women on the left and men on the right.

When it was Emery's turn to be sorted, one of the two officers in charge of the sorting process looked them over, taking in the short, undercut hair, the eyeliner and the colourful clothing, and barked, "What are you?"

Alice saw Emery stiffen, but they kept their composure and replied calmly, "Non-binary."

"Huh?" The police officer turned to a colleague. "What do I do with this one, then?"

The second officer – a short, stocky guy with his face scrunched up like a raisin – walked forward until his nose was half an inch from Emery's. "What. Are. You!" he shouted, spittle landing on Emery's cheeks.

Emery took a step backwards, ran their sleeve over their face and repeated, as calmly as before, "Non-binary."

In a flash, the officer drew his right foot back and kicked Emery hard in the groin. Emery yelled and collapsed onto their knees, holding their crotch. Alice, Matilda and several others screamed.

"You fucking pig!" Alice yelled at the police officer as she ran towards Emery, who was still crumpled on the floor. The policeman stopped her in her tracks by grabbing a handful of her T-shirt.

"You want some too, bitch?" he barked in her face. Alice felt a wave of rage surge through her and clenched her fists, but managed to stop herself from striking the officer in the face, knowing that she would only be making things worse for herself and possibly for everyone else if she did. Shaking, she tore herself out of the policeman's grip – her T-shirt tearing in the process – and made her way back to her place in the line, hugging herself to minimise exposure through the rip in her top. Matilda leaned into her, sobbing again.

The officer grabbed a handful of Emery's shirt and pulled them to their feet. Emery was shaking but silent. "I think we can safely say this one's male, Sandra," the policeman called to his colleague as he shoved Emery into the men's group. Both officers guffawed, and Alice felt the sting of tears at the edge of her eyes. She squeezed her eyes tight and swallowed until she was confident that the threat had passed, knowing that any sign of weakness would make her an easy target.

When the sorting process was complete, each group was bustled into a cell. Two police officers stood at the door of the cell, stripping the prisoners of all their belongings and forcing them to remove all jewellery, belts and shoelaces. Once inside the dark, damp cell, there was nothing to do but huddle and wait.

About an hour later, the door to the cell opened again and the policewoman from the sorting entered, holding a small tablet. She began asking everyone in turn for their name, date of birth and address. Alice was sitting on the floor between Cora and Matilda, and it was Matilda that the officer addressed first.

"You down there, with the glasses. What's your name?" she barked.

"M-Matilda S-Stone," came the reply, barely more than a whisper.

"Date of birth?"

"S-Second of February, 2001."

"Address?"

"55 Birchall Lane, London, E2 0GX."

"You?"

It took Alice a few seconds to realise that the officer had moved on to her. "No comment," she said, and Cora did the same. Alice exchanged a look with her friend and decided to wait until the policewoman had left again before she said anything.

As soon as the door of the cell had banged shut again, Alice and Cora turned towards Matilda. "Stone?" they asked in unison. "As in Harold Stone?" Cora added.

Matilda pursed her lips and nodded. "I didn't want to tell you," she whispered. "I thought you might not want to hang out with me. Harold Stone is my uncle."

SATURDAY

What made this gruelling, awful day even worse for Alice was the memory she had of visiting this building on a field trip in her first year at SOAS. Neepa Acharjee, the PhD student who had taught Introduction to Law and Legal Processes during Alice's very first term at the university, had wanted to do something fun for their last session, and had organised a visit to the Central Criminal Court – which most people call 'The Old Bailey' – and the Royal Courts of Justice.

A retired teacher and local history enthusiast had taken the class around the two buildings, pointing out the stunning frescoes, marble pillars and statues and regaling the students with tales of the most notorious criminals to have been sentenced here, from Jack the Ripper to the Kray twins. Alice remembered snapping a picture on her phone of the phrase *The law of the wise is a fountain of life*, which was painted above a doorway in the Grand Hall of the Old Bailey, and which the tour guide had told them came from the Bible.

Today, Alice and her fellow defendants hadn't been taken to the courtroom through frescoed hallways, but pushed and pulled through a narrow passage which led directly from a side street to the dock. After spending the night in the holding cells of Belgravia Police Station, they probably smelled as bad as the inmates of Newgate Prison, which had been housed in the bowels of the court building for centuries and had smelled so foul that the judges had taken to wearing flower posies to hide the smell, as Alice recalled from her tour.

At the time of her field trip, she had dismissed the fact that bouquets were still found in the building's courtrooms in the present day as just another quirk of the English judiciary, like the wearing of wigs and gowns in Crown courts. Today, as she obeyed the usher's command of "All rise!", Alice fixed the small jug of purple carnations on the judge's bench with a glare of intense hatred.

District Judge Mark Eggart was tall and thin, with a ramrod-straight spine, pale skin and a grim expression framed by deep wrinkles. Despite her three years of legal education, Alice almost expected him to pick up a gavel and bang it, and had to remind herself that English judges didn't have gavels at all.

"Why are we even here?" Cora whispered to Alice as the solicitors and the scores of journalists and members of the public who lined the public gallery took their seats again. Alice shook her head in response. Having spent the night at the police station with no phone, she had no way of knowing for sure why all those accused of inciting yesterday's public assembly and failing to comply with the police order to disperse had been taken to the Old Bailey, which was a Crown court, when the crime they had been charged with was a summary offence - at least the duty sergeant had told them that much - and should have been heard at a magistrates' court.

Alice suspected that the Queen wanted to make a public show of their prosecution and had therefore requested that the hearing and trial be held at this grand, historic home of criminal punishment, rather than at the more spartan and anonymous Westminster Magistrates' Court. Surely, if the monarch asks you to hold a hearing in a certain place, or at a certain time, you comply.

"This is the hearing for case number 18WM05021202," the clerk announced. "The Crown versus Ali and others, District Judge Mark Eggart presiding. All defendants have been charged with organising a public assembly and knowingly failing to comply with a condition imposed under section 14 of the Public Order Act 1986. On summary conviction, all defendants will be liable to imprisonment for a term not exceeding three months, or a fine not exceeding level four on the standard scale, or both. Defendant Deshad Abdul Ali, how do you plead?"

Deshad stood straight in the dock, though Alice could see his hands twitching slightly at his side as he answered, "Not guilty, sir." He sat down again and their solicitor, Safia, shot him a sympathetic look.

"Defendant Eda Nur Bashir, how do you plead?"

"Not guilty, sir."

"Defendant Emery Bloom, how do you plead?"

"Not guilty, sir." Alice squeezed her friend's hand as Emery sat down next to where she was standing.

"Defendant Cora García Gómez, how do you plead?"

"Not guilty, sir."

"Defendant Alice Nokutenda Mushonga, how do you plead?"

Alice took a deep breath. "Not guilty, sir," she announced. As she lowered herself into her seat, she could feel her legs trembling under her. Although the five of them had decided to hire Safia together after she had been recommended by the protest law firm whose phone number had been on the bust card, and had all decided to follow her advice and enter a not guilty plea, Alice had worried that some of her friends might change their mind. The fact that all defendants had pleaded 'not guilty' would hopefully present a united front at the trial, where Safia was planning to argue that their failure to comply with the police order had been due to circumstances beyond the protesters' control.

Given that neither Alice nor any of the other defendants had any previous convictions, they were all released on bail. As she left the courtroom, Alice spotted Matilda coming out of the room next door, where the hearing for those who had only been charged with participating in an unlawful assembly – as opposed to organising one or inciting others to join – had been held. The two women shared an awkward glance and a brief, chaste hug before joining their friends for the trek back to the police station, where they collected the belongings which had been taken from them the previous day.

As soon as she turned her phone on, Alice saw an email from Jammer and Barrett: *Dear Ms Mushonga, we regret to inform you that due to your involvement in a recent episode of public disorder we have had no choice but to withdraw your offer of employment with us in order to safeguard our firm's reputation.*

"Shit!" Alice said to Emery as they walked together towards the Tube. "I should never have agreed to that bloody interview!"

The next notification to come through was a text from Fran: *Are you and Emery okay? I was awake all night with Ben and didn't hear anybody come in next door.*

We all got arrested, Alice replied. *Just had our hearing. And I lost my job.*

Alice was hoping for a sympathetic response, but she heard nothing back. When she and Emery finally got home, the curtains in Fran's living room were drawn. It was only hours later, when Alice was getting ready to go to bed, that her phone pinged again with a text from Fran: *Sorry. Now Milo has chickenpox too. Had to pick him up early from nursery. I know you and Emery are probably shaken up, but I just can't do it all.*

* * *

The Queen was sitting in her study and enjoying a novel when her equerry entered the room and announced that Mr Maloney wanted an audience. Maloney barged in, or at least it felt that way to Isabel when the normally subdued and restrained former Ravenmaster strode in behind the equerry, standing straight and tall until the moment came to bow his head to the Queen. He was wearing his red uniform again, which was surprising given his resignation the previous day. Isabel sensed that besides his change in demeanour there was something else different about him. It took her a few moments to realise that, for the first time since this whole ordeal had begun, Maloney was smiling.

He was clasping a small envelope tightly, and from the way his lips were twitching Isabel could tell that he was bursting to say something and was struggling to stick to protocol and not speak until spoken to. Isabel gestured for him to take a seat. "Do you have news for me, Mr Maloney?" she prompted.

"Yes, Your Majesty." Almost beaming, Maloney handed her the envelope. Inside it was a printout of an email addressed to the Ravenmaster from a Lynn Rector of County Down Rare Birds.

Dear Mr Maloney, it read, *I am pleased to confirm that all six young birds which were born to our breeding pair of ravens earlier this Spring have survived the brooding phase. The fledglings should be ready to disperse in about three months, and it would be our honour and pleasure to offer the entire brood to Her Majesty the Queen to replace the lost ravens of the Tower of London.*

An unusual sense of calm spread through Isabel's body, from her core all the way to her fingers and toes. Smiling, she folded up the printout and set it aside on a coffee table. "I presume you would like your job back, Mr Maloney?"

Maloney bowed his head. "If Your Majesty will allow it."

"I will. Good work, Ravenmaster."

"Thank you, ma'am." Maloney smiled broadly, then started, the smile freezing on his lips. "But, Your Majesty, I've only just remembered that I don't have a place of work anymore."

"Speak to my equerry on your way out," Isabel replied after pondering for a few seconds. "Tell him that I asked for him to show you around the palace gardens. You can have a look for the best place to house the new ravens, and you'll have three months to get everything ready for them."

"Thank you, Your Majesty." Maloney stood up, bowed, took a step backwards and turned to leave. Just before he reached the door he turned back. "Your Majesty, should I ask Major Phillips to get me a different uniform, since I won't be a Yeoman Warder anymore?"

The Queen thought for a few moments. "No, keep your Beefeater uniform. People go on tours of the gardens sometimes. It will be a good reminder of the Tower and all it stood for."

THREE MONTHS LATER

"Here they are, Your Majesty." Maloney bowed his head as he presented the Queen with a large golden cage containing the six young ravens he had picked up from Belfast a couple of days before.

"Is this secure, Mr Maloney?" Isabel asked, taking the cage gingerly in her hands and examining the lock on the door.

"Absolutely, Your Majesty. I tested it three times."

"Good. Well, hop in, then."

"Ma'am?" The Ravenmaster looked confused as he stared at the gilded exterior of the Gold State Coach.

"Hop in," Isabel repeated. "You can mind this cage. It's always a very bumpy ride in this coach, and I don't want the cage cracking open. We've had enough ravens fly away from us, haven't we?"

"Y-Yes, Your Majesty. Thank you, ma'am." Maloney pulled himself up inside the coach and sat on the other side from the Queen, with the ravens' cage in the middle. A footman closed the door behind him, and at a signal from the Queen the coach started moving.

Isabel looked back at the ruins of the White Tower, which they were now leaving behind. She never would have thought that a castle which had been built by William the Conqueror and had lasted for so many centuries would crumble to dust during her reign, under her very eyes. It spooked her to think that the legend of the ravens had, in part, come true: as the ravens had left, the tower had fallen. But so what? The other half of the prophecy, the half that really mattered, had not materialised. No tragedy had befallen the kingdom, had it? The military threat had turned out to be non-existent, and her ambassadors to Venezuela and Russia had managed to smooth things over with a few well placed gifts and official apologies. Besides, Stone was proving to be a much more useful Prime Minister than the Queen had anticipated. After the prorogation protests, he had hurried to relay Isabel's orders to the Home Secretary, resulting in a three-month ban on public processions around Buckingham Palace – except today's one, of course.

As she thought back through the events of the previous three months, Isabel waved at the crowd. People had turned out in great numbers to see their Queen in her golden carriage as she transported the new set of ravens from the ruins of the White Tower to their newly built enclosure in the gardens of Buckingham Palace. Isabel herself had charted a carefully studied route, which would take them north past the Old Bailey and then back south past 10 Downing Street and the Houses of Parliament, finally approaching Buckingham Palace from the same direction the protesters had come from three months previously.

The journey took a long time in the horse-drawn carriage, but Isabel enjoyed looking at the scores of people lining both sides of the road and waving at the coach as it ambled past them. Every time they passed a major landmark, the crowd – encouraged by two dozen strategically placed palace footmen – began to sing.

* * *

Alice scanned the courtroom until she saw Matilda.

Her ex-girlfriend locked eyes with Alice, smiled and nodded in encouragement. Alice was grateful for Matilda's support, and seeing her sweet smile again – a smile which went all the way up to her eyes, even in a tense situation like this one – almost made her regret breaking up with Matilda when they had met up a couple of days after their hearings. But once Matilda's father had got her exonerated with a well placed call to a former Navy comrade who was now high up in the justice system, Alice had realised that she and this young woman had too little in common to last as a couple. Matilda was the Prime Minister's niece, for goodness' sake! Besides, if Alice was found guilty, spending three months in prison wouldn't help their relationship any.

"Defendant Alice Nokutenda Mushonga." The judge's voice brought Alice back to the present. This was it – verdict time. Alice's heart started racing, and as she stood to receive her verdict her legs trembled.

"This court finds the defendant guilty. The defendant is hereby sentenced to three months' imprisonment and a fine of two thousand, four hundred pounds."

If the ravens leave the Tower of London, the Tower will fall, and a great misfortune will befall the kingdom. Strangely, this was the first thought that crossed Alice's mind as soon as she heard her sentence. While she and her friends from Students for Real Democracy had been busy organising their protests, the ravens had fled the Tower of London one by one, and the White Tower had crumbled to dust. And look at where the country was now: what little democratic governance there had once been had been taken away from them. As for Alice herself, she was unemployed and now bound for prison. Misfortunes all round.

While Alice had been thinking about all of this, the judge had sentenced everybody else to the same fate. Just as he finished speaking, a distant sound drifted into the courtroom from the open window, worming its way into Alice's brain. It was a melody - quite a slow, solemn one - and Alice knew she'd heard it before, but she couldn't immediately place it.

While the judge explained his reasons for choosing the sentence he had, the sound moved closer and closer. Finally, the judge rose to leave the room, and a police officer took hold of Alice's arm. As she felt cold metal encircle her wrists and heard the handcuffs click shut, Alice managed to make out a few words from the song:

Send her victorious,
Happy and glorious,
Long to reign over us,
God save the Queen!

The royals' supposed lack of power and influence is the most pernicious of all public fantasies.

Joan Smith, from *Down With The Royals*
(Biteback Publishing, 2015)

Acknowledgements

I would like to thank Dr Yvonne Battle-Felton and everyone at Litfest's New Writing North West 2021 fiction workshop for giving me feedback on the beginning of this book.

I would also like to thank my partner Bodhi Hunt and my friend Håvard Skogerbø for story consultancy and support.

Finally, thanks once again to my friend Stephanie Cage for her writing advice.

About the Author

Marta Pacini is the author of *The (Un)lawful Killing of Daniel Brown* and the pioneering founder of radical independent publisher Disturbance Press. She wrote her first story at age nine, won her first literary prize at age sixteen and was selected to participate in the New Writing North West workshop at Lancaster LitFest 2021.

Marta is a roamer who currently lays her hat in Accrington, Lancashire.

Find out more about Marta Pacini at
martapacinibooks.com, or contact her at
info@martapacinibooks.com.

About Disturbance Press

Disturbance Press is a new independent publishing house based in Lancashire, UK.

We publish thought-provoking fiction for both adults and young people, and aim to bring stories with a social and environmental justice focus into the mainstream reading culture.

Unapologetically leftist, we aspire to create a community of engaged readers and writers.

Find us at disturbancepress.co.uk.

www.ingramcontent.com/pod-product-compliance
Ingram Content Group UK Ltd.
Pitfield, Milton Keynes, MK11 3LW, UK
UKHW040004200726
13854UKWH00001B/29